EVERYWHERE, ALWAYS

JENNIFER ANN SHORE

Copyright © 2021 by Jennifer Ann Shore

All rights reserved.

No part of this book may be reproduced in any form or by any electronic or mechanical means, including information storage and retrieval systems, without written permission from the author, except for the use of brief quotations in a book review.

Print ISBN: 978-1-7360672-3-9

For Marmie,
I love you so

ONE

I don't see it coming.

It's the moment that's going to end one life and change another so completely that things will start being referred to as the "before" and "after" of what happens.

At least, mentally—because it's rarely spoken about out loud, and when it is, it's with a type of stabbing pain that forces a person to think of anything and everything else as soon as possible.

For now, I'm unaware.

Why would I expect anything to happen?

It's just like any other Saturday, perfectly boring, long, and quiet.

Ordinary, really, starting with a large bowl of sugary cereal that's a little stale. I like to pretend it's by choice that the marshmallows are a weird, mostly tough texture, but I let them soak up the milk for as long as my grumbling stomach will allow until I scarf it all down in record time.

I think that one day, maybe, I'll be one of those people

who can take the time to enjoy the meal. Like the types of people at the restaurant I work at who have long conversations while savoring every morsel of rich garlic butter, freshly grated parmesan cheese, and velvety soft noodles.

But for now, when it comes to inhaling calories, I consider myself to be very practical or maybe a little utilitarian.

I only know the word "utilitarian" because I jammed it into my brain before retaking the SAT over the summer, and it's one of the many new vocabulary words that has stuck since—well, that one and my personal favorite of "capricious," but I haven't had a chance to put that one to use yet.

This line of thinking makes me want to be productive before my shift at the restaurant, so I sigh as I drop my bowl in the sink, resolving to wash it later, and grab my backpack from the hook by the door.

I make myself comfortable on the sole worn chair on our back porch.

It only takes a few minutes of balancing my textbook on my knees for me to curse whoever invented calculus.

"You wearing sunscreen, Avery?"

My mother asks me the question while clutching a cup of coffee like it's the only thing that's keeping her going—and frankly, it might be. She pulled a double shift yesterday, from open to close, which is great for maximizing tips but not so great for one's physical and mental health.

All the sacrifices she has made and continues to make for me melt away the frustration I feel as I scratch out my equation for the third time.

She has given up everything to be the best mother to

me, creating a life for us all on her own, and I just want to be able to do right by her someday.

She has made it clear I have no obligation to her other than to do what I want to do—whether it's going to college or joining the Peace Corps or any other random examples she pulls out of thin air whenever we discuss my future.

I love that she supports me so wholly, but I can't imagine living without helping her find and follow her own dreams.

She's been the best example of strength and independence I could ask for in a mother-slash-role-model, but it hurts my heart to imagine her eventually being old and gray and still carrying heavy trays of drinks and uncorking wine for people who look down their noses at her.

So, I don't complain, even when I feel totally overwhelmed by juggling school and working twenty hours a week.

With me a few weeks into my senior year, we're so close to starting the next phase of our lives, and I'm just celebrating the win that we both had this morning off to recharge.

For her, it means sleeping in until two o'clock, and for me, it means soaking up the last rays of the summer sun and hoping that somehow the rays will make me some sort of math genius.

Plus, my tan is practically nonexistent, and I'm not going to block out the last hope I have of getting free Vitamin D infused into my skin by slathering on smelly, pricy sunscreen.

"Yep, definitely," I call back, then using one of my other vocabulary words, I add, "Diligently!"

"Uh huh," she says with a chuckle that reveals her skepticism.

I smile to myself, appreciating the fact that she knows I'm lying but doesn't call me out on it.

I see so many mothers and daughters at each other's throats as I seat them or refill their water glasses at work, and each time, I feel even more like I won the maternal lottery.

If only it came with millions of dollars...

But her gentle reminder is enough to get me to give in to what she wants—me in the house, not getting burned—and she knows it.

Still, I pretend that the reason I'm heading inside is because my brain refuses to cooperate on my calculus any longer.

"Leftovers for lunch," my mother says as she pulls two bowls of last night's pasta out of the microwave.

"Thank you," I say, joining her at our scuffed-up kitchen table.

It, like most of our furniture, came with the one-bedroom apartment. It's smaller than our last one but more centrally located, a huge advantage for our commute last winter in the Western Pennsylvanian snowfall.

"What's wrong with this one?" I ask, stirring my fork around to release some of the steam.

Working at an Italian restaurant means we dine on a lot of their food that was either purchased with our employee discount or snagged when customers have it sent back to the kitchen. I've eaten so much garlic that I wouldn't be surprised if it's permanently embedded into my bloodstream somehow.

"It appalled the customer that we garnished it with parsley," she explains. "Apparently on her two-week trip to Naples last year, they used basil."

I snort. "Do they even have fettuccine alfredo in Italy?"

"No idea," she says. "We can find out in the future when I retire and buy a villa there."

She does this regularly, imagining that we have a grand future life ahead of us.

I think it's because it's better than acknowledging our reality, which is near-constant moving around the outskirts of Pittsburgh into cheaper apartments while chasing more lucrative pay.

We've been here for almost a year, the longest we've ever stayed in one place, but I can't say that I've made too much of an effort to put down roots—I go to school, work, do homework, fall asleep to reruns, and start the process all over again.

The stability has been nice, and we've been ahead on our bills long enough to build out a small savings account.

She wants to put it toward college for me, but I'm not totally sold on the idea just yet—plus, I find immense satisfaction in watching the numbers tick up.

It's one of the few things we disagree on, and we're both firm on our opinions. She says I need to focus on building some great, magnificent future career, not worrying about paying for groceries.

We eat in near-silence, but it's something I don't even notice until we're halfway through the meal.

I smile at her, mouth closed because it's full of noodles, and she returns it.

I'm pretty sure we could have an entire day of conversations without actually speaking, a well-practiced art that comes from years of us taking care of each other.

Once we've both finished, I clean up my bowl from earlier and our containers, which make up the majority of our "dishes," then we make quick work of getting ourselves ready.

My mom braids her hair back, and seeing my jealousy at her ability to do so—it's something I've never quite figured out—she asks if she can do mine.

I nod, and she arranges my pin straight black hair by twisting and moving the strands until they're braided together and then she secures it with an elastic.

With our hair back and in our matching black slacks and white button-down shirts, we look closer in age than ever. Even though we don't look very much alike, we regularly get mistaken for being sisters rather than mother and daughter. It annoyed me when I was younger, but after comprehending how much it meant for a single mom in her late thirties to get a compliment, reversing her age after being robbed of her youth, I'm happy to be likened to it.

"I have a good feeling about tonight," she says, sliding in the driver's seat.

She is an eternal optimist, a trait that I'm pretty sure didn't get passed down to me genetically.

Then again, her brand of positivity usually encompasses things like the weather or getting left a big tip, not the moment my life gets violently thrown into a tailspin.

"You always have a good feeling about something," I remind her, buckling my seatbelt as she pulls out of the parking spot.

"And there's nothing wrong with that," she says, definitively.

"If you always have a good feeling, then you're setting the bar for that to be the norm," I argue, but I'm unable to suppress the grin on my face. "Then instead of a normal day being fine, we won't know what days are actually good because we have to achieve greatness for it to be spectacular."

"Then I guess we're just going to have to go for 'great' and 'spectacular' instead."

I pause, mulling over her words. "I like that. But I'll flip through my vocab notecards to see if there's a better adjective for us to work toward."

She laughs. "Works for me."

We cruise down the straight, wide road that's lined with chain restaurants and stores, and I find comfort in how after this long in one place, they seem familiar to me.

I used to keep track of how many shifts I worked as a hostess and my mom worked as a server at the restaurant, but after the hundredth, which we celebrated by splitting a slice of cheesecake, I stopped counting.

"I saw Adam making eyes at you last night," she says lightly, tapping on the steering wheel as we idle at a red light.

At this, I roll my eyes.

She's always convinced that some guy somewhere is interested in me, but I think she's overcompensating because I'm too preoccupied with other things to have a boyfriend or do all the silly things teenagers are supposed to do.

"He just likes to keep track of how many people are

coming in the restaurant," I argue. "Trying to get a feel of how busy the kitchen's going to be and whatnot."

"Well, he doesn't do that during Macy's shift, I can assure you."

My cheeks grow red and hot as I sense her knowing smile. "I'm too busy for a relationship."

"Who says you need to have a relationship with him?"

"Mom!" I laugh. "Shouldn't you be advocating for me to stay on track with school, work, and college applications?"

The light turns green, and she chuckles as she speeds up through the intersection. "Maybe it's time we both started worrying a little less and living a little—"

The sound of her voice, the soft, singsong tone I've heard every single day of my life, cuts off, and it's replaced with its antithesis.

Time as I know it suspends, and everything somehow moves in slow motion but at twice the normal speed.

One second I'm glancing over at my mother, and in the next, I see a black SUV coming straight for us.

Ignoring the red light of the traffic signal, the car accelerates, plowing through the intersection at full speed into my mother's side of the car.

My body jolts from the impact, and I close my eyes on instinct, as if that will protect me from the damage.

I squeeze my lids tightly so I don't see the repercussions just yet, but I hear them.

And then, I feel them.

The loud, violent sound of metal crunching only magnifies the physical impact of the collision. I don't know if it's the airbag deploying on my mother's side or the rest of the destruction that causes the echo in my ears.

My seatbelt cuts into my neck, attempting to hold me in place as I'm forced sideways into my door, cracking my skull against the window.

The force propels us until we're slammed into a waiting car on the other side of the street, but by the time I get my bearings, my ears ring loud enough to drown out everything else.

I peel my eyes open, fighting against tunneling vision.

"Mom," I yell or scream or whisper.

I can't tell which because the sound is muffled, like we're underwater instead of in our old Honda.

The pain of turning my head is so intense I nearly pass out, but I press on even though the movement of my neck sends streaks of fire down my spine. I fight through it, only to be met with a devastation greater than anything I've ever experienced in my seventeen years of life.

My mother—my best friend, my confidant, my person—is gone.

Part of me dies right along with her.

TWO

I don't quite understand the passing of time, but I do know that I'm alive.

It's like I'm getting flashes of consciousness—the jolt of movement, the murmurs of chatter above me, the sirens, the beeping of machines, the pain. I'm somehow distant from it all, stuck in that feeling of being asleep yet awake, and I'm just out of it enough where I can't piece together reality but am cognizant of sounds and my own feelings and needs.

My mother always said that the best days of our lives are ahead of us—we just have to keep working to make them happen.

But I'm fairly certain that the best days of my life are behind me and that everything ahead is going to be complete agony.

It's been the two of us for my entire life, looking after each other, sharing meals, and trying to get ahead. She has always been my biggest fan, supporter, and critic, always pushing me to work harder and smarter, wanting nothing but the best for me.

And now she is dead.

I don't bother with "passed away" or other softer descriptions because it feels almost unfair of me to color the truth, and somehow, it makes me feel more in control if I'm direct with the momentous—another vocabulary word —truth.

She's past tense now.

My mother will continue to exist in the memories and few photographs I have of her, but the mental image of her lifeless eyes boring into my tear-blurred ones is something I will undoubtedly carry with me for the rest of my life.

I keep getting flashes of the accident, but the physical pain momentarily overpowers my emotional trauma. Every single part of my body aches, but my right arm and side of my face pulsate with the steady burn of soreness.

As I come back to consciousness, my senses grow stronger.

The sheets are surprisingly soft on my fingertips, and a floral scent masks the bleach one. I hear the steady beeping of a heart rate monitor, the low murmur of cable news, and voices arguing just far enough away that I can make out the tone, not the words.

Thoughts of my mother bloodied and unbreathing floods back in, and I decide I need to push away that memory, knowing I can only do it by trying to cope with this reality.

I visualize myself packing it up in a suitcase and storing it in the far back corner of my mind—the same one where all the embarrassing moments of my early teenage years are stashed—and hoping it won't escape without voluntarily unpacking it myself.

My eyelids weigh one thousand pounds, but I manage to slowly force them open.

In the many hours of my life I've watched reruns of medical dramas, I know that most patients wake up bleary-eyed and confused, asking their doctors what happened before loved ones rush toward them in complete relief and hopefulness.

Unfortunately, I have a near-perfect recollection of the events but no people at my bedside.

I try to call for a nurse, or anyone, but my voice is hoarse to the point where it barely exists. My entire mouth is so dry that I can't even generate enough moisture to wet my cracked lips with my tongue.

Physically, I'm weak, but mentally, I think I'm strong—at least until I blink, taking in my surroundings, and for the first time since the accident, confusion rolls over me.

I expect to be in one of many beds in an emergency room, or at least have a roommate in a curtained-off area like the one I experienced when I was seven years old and my appendix ruptured. But the room I'm in is bigger than the bedroom my mother and I share in our apartment—and it's complete with a private bathroom and a decent sized sitting area.

I turn my attention back to my sore body to assess the damage. It doesn't feel broken; although, the wrapping and bandages on my right hand and arm indicate I might be just a little bit, but the hanging bag of fluid is probably pumping medicine into my system to help stave off the worst of the pain.

Suddenly, the crack in the wooden door to the room widens.

I recoil at the brightness that floods in from the hallway. After a flew blinks, my eyes adjust and take in an older gentleman, wearing dark blue scrubs and a white coat.

He offers me a smile that I can't even fathom returning.

"Good, you're awake."

Is it good?

I can't decide, but I definitely feel like falling back to sleep all over again and not waking up.

"Avery, I'm Dr. Ross," he says slowly, anticipating that my brain needs time to catch it. "You're in the hospital after a nasty accident, but you're fine. We're taking good care of you."

I understand why he says this to me. But his words don't offer me any comfort because they're just the things doctors are supposed to say to patients—to reassure them all is fine, even though their lives have spiraled into absolute free fall.

"I'm going to check you over," Dr. Ross tells me. "Is that okay?"

This time, I try to respond in the form of a nod, but I'm pretty sure my head only moves one single centimeter, if even that much.

The doctor mutters to himself while he checks my bandages and monitors, then shines a light in my eyes that causes me to gasp and flinch away from him.

"You're looking good, Avery, all things considered. Can you tell me how much pain you're in?"

I almost laugh at the absurdity of that question. In fact, I should burst out in a fit of giggles or cry or do anything other than stare at him, but I've compartmentalized my emotions, and I'll be damned if I open up the floodgates in front of this complete stranger, even if the pain is so high on the scale it doesn't register.

"Water," is what I decide to croak out, pleading with my eyes as my voice fails me.

He obliges my request, pouring a glass of water—in an actual glass, I note—which I accept with a shaking left hand.

The liquid feels divine in my parched mouth, and I greedily suck in as much as I can, spilling a good amount on myself in the process.

"You must have some questions."

"Yes," I say, finding my voice a little more. "My mother—"

"You are very lucky." He brushes past my attempt to acknowledge her death. "You've been in and out for a while now, but it's a good sign that you're awake."

"How long?" I ask, but again, he continues on.

"No internal damage aside from a somewhat moderate concussion. You might have some symptoms like nausea and light sensitivity that stay with you for a few weeks. Other than that, some cuts, bumps, and bruises from the impact and broken glass that will all heal just fine. But this—"

He gingerly reaches for my right hand, where my pinky and ring fingers are taped together.

"—is a very slight fracture on your small finger."

"Displaced?" I ask him.

He cocks an eyebrow. "Non-displaced."

The bone is broken, but it hasn't shifted out of place

enough to cause concern. No surgery required, thankfully.

"Are you a med student?" Dr. Ross asks.

One look at my chart should tell him unless I'm some sort of teenage prodigy, I'm far too young for that.

"I hoped to be someday," I tell him.

"Well, you're off to a good start," he says, offering me a tight smile.

It was always a thought in the back of my mind that if my mother and I saved enough, I could go into the medical field in some aspect. I don't strictly love medical dramas for the angst, hot doctors, and love stories.

Even before I took the SATs, I researched a number of different colleges and trade schools on the computers at school during my lunch hour, and it seemed like in the near future, nursing school might be a good option.

My mother wanted me to dream bigger, to take her optimism and drive into a future without limits, but I was too practical for that. I'd already earmarked scholarships, started the application process for a few programs, and attempted to figure out the best way for it.

Now, it all seems so meaningless.

We worked together—just the two of us—to build a future, and now what? I'm just supposed to carry on without her?

The thought makes my throat itch.

Emotions threaten to spill out, and I hold them all in, swallowing repeatedly until tears stop forming and I can breathe without feeling like my lungs are constricted.

I raise my good arm to wipe my cheeks, but my fingers hit a bandage. I trace the material, noting that it runs from the side of my eye all the way down to my jaw.

"Careful," Dr. Ross warns. "We just removed the stitches."

He leans over me and slowly peels off the adhesive, commenting on how good the wound looks. There's trepidation in his voice that makes me panic, and I'm already imagining the worst.

"Can I see it?" I ask.

All things considered, it's pretty juvenile and vain to care about my appearance, but at the very least, I always hoped to be able to recognize my own reflection. I guess it's not that surprising of a request—and one he must have anticipated—because he reaches over and pulls a hand mirror off the side table.

Everything about my face is as I recall, minus the angry line running the length of my cheek.

It's dotted with redness, where I assume the stitches were, and the cut itself is a little puckered. The cut is hideous and overlarge, and it's going to be the first thing I see in the mirror from now on, a constant reminder of the day I lost my mother.

Even worse, I can imagine her hand on my cheek, how she gently rested it on that exact spot so many times when giving me advice or praise.

She'll never be able to do that again.

I choke back the sob that comes with that realization, and the doctor mistakes my reaction for dissatisfaction over what I see.

"I can assure you that it's the worst it will be now, with the swelling and the redness, but if it doesn't heal up to your liking, we can get a plastics consult set."

I can't muster up the energy to find humor in that

suggestion.

Dr. Ross doesn't know that I don't really have enough money to cover the cost of him, let alone anything cosmetic.

I'm already dreading the hours and hours I'm going to spend on the phone with the insurance company, begging and pleading my case. I'm not sure they're going to love that I somehow am in a very swanky private room, which reminds me of the first thing I noticed when I woke up.

"Why am I here?" I interrupt Dr. Ross's long spiel about aftercare for the wound that I tuned out a few minutes ago. "Which hospital is this?"

I look at the badge that's clipped to the front of his scrubs, taking in his name and ID number easily enough, but I don't recognize the name.

"Carter-Churchill Medical, the best hospital in the five boroughs."

He says that as if it's a tagline I'm supposed to recognize, like one of those jingles in a credit report commercial, but I draw a blank.

"I don't know..." I pause, trying not to sound like a totally uncultured idiot, even if my trauma does offer me a little leeway. "Where is it located?" My tone is forceful enough that it's obvious confusion, not some accident-related memory loss.

There are a few hospitals in downtown Pittsburgh, but I know all of those names and locations—certainly I would have seen something on the news if they were bought out or changed the name. Plus, there's an emergency room not too far from the restaurant, so I don't understand why I'm not there.

"68th and York."

"Is that some sort of code?" I ask.

"You're not—" He stops himself, as if he's remembering which patient I am, and clears his throat.

It's silent for a few beats as he finishes up reapplying the bandage to my face, then he steps back and sits in the chair beside my bed, trying to make his demeanor soft and warm.

"I was hoping that Social Services would be here to explain, but I'm afraid I have some bad news."

"My mother is dead," I say plainly.

He swallows, a little put off by my directness. "She wasn't in any pain," he says, as if that's supposed to comfort me. "And we're going to get everything figured out from here on out. All you have to do is focus on getting better."

He stands to leave.

I don't know if he wants to put the burden of the rest of this conversation on someone else or give me time to compose myself, but I pull up the sheet and sink back against the pillows.

"Let me go see if I can track down our contact for you," he says, reaching for the door. "Just try to rest in the meantime. Sleep will help heal you."

I wait until he's gone and I'm left mostly in darkness to unleash the wailing cry I've been holding inside.

My mother would hate that I've broken down, that I'm not holding onto her false optimism and good feelings. But the weight of this reality hits my chest just as hard as that other car slammed into us, and I need to let it all out, just for a little while.

THREE

I spend the better part of an hour sobbing into a pillow.

I've never felt such grief and numbness in this magnitude before, and I am unsure how to navigate it. Everything hurts now, but I don't think it's just because the medication is wearing off.

Carol from Social Services is a bright-eyed, thirty-something woman in a brown dress. She has kind eyes, and her look of determination screams of good intentions—but I'm not sure I'm ready to be on the receiving end of those just yet.

Even though he seemed to want no part of the discussion about my dead mother, for some reason, Dr. Ross lingers nearby. I'll take the show of support because it somehow feels less intense to have a buffer, even if he's shifting on his feet and staring out the window.

I mean, if I had my preference it would be to be left alone to wallow, but I might be all out of tears because I feel utterly spent and completely empty. No need to hide my emotions now—I have nothing left to give.

In fact, I barely listen to Carol as she speaks until she explains that the drunk driver also "lost his life" in the accident.

He didn't just lose his life—he stole another, but I don't have the energy to get annoyed at that expression.

I stare at the blank wall, trying to process her words as she continues talking about funeral arrangements for my mother and reaffirming the "we're all in this together" vibe Dr. Ross tried to set the stage for earlier.

"Do you have questions?" Carol asks once her spiel is complete.

It's clear that she's waiting for me to respond in some way, to cry, scream, or do anything other than lay like a vegetable, even though that's all I want to do. But I can't collapse into myself.

I feel weirdly lucid and rational at the moment, and maybe it's some leftover adrenaline or just resolve overpowering helplessness, but most of all, I'm practical. There's no one left to fight for me, which means I need to take control of the situation and figure out how to move forward.

"What happens next?" I ask her.

Carol reaches out and squeezes my good hand. "Whatever happens, I am here for you," she reassures me once again. "I'm overseeing your case. There are several programs and options for teenagers in situations like yours—"

"I'm almost eighteen," I say before she can go any further. "I can take care of myself."

She shakes her head. "It feels like it, I know, but in the State of New York's eyes, you're a minor for nine more months."

I blink. "I'm sorry, did you say the State of *New York*?"

Carol glares at Dr. Ross, seemingly irritated that this is new information to me.

"You were flown out of your hometown hospital the day after your accident," she explains.

It seems a little extreme for a concussion, broken finger, and facial gash, but I tuck that thought away for more pressing matters—like how I'm going to stay out of the system, get back home, finish out high school, and scrape enough cash together to figure out my post-graduation plans.

"What are my options, then?" I ask.

She takes a breath. "Unfortunately, your mother did not leave a will or guardianship agreement in place, so you'll either need to be placed with your relatives or in foster care."

"But if I'm a minor, can't I file for emancipation or something?" I argue, recalling that word from an old episode of *House*. "I can live on my own, and we have a little money saved to pay for the next few months of rent."

"You have a very proactive spirit, but to argue before a court that you're able to take care of yourself on your own income with school...it's a stretch at this point. At the very least, you'll need some time to recover and to get back on your feet."

"I can drop out of school and get my GED," I say, but I immediately cringe when I do, knowing my mother would've wanted me to stay in school and cross the stage in a cap and gown.

But she's not here to decide for me anymore, and I need to do what I think is best.

"Let's not get ahead of ourselves," Carol says, stopping the plea that's already forming in my head. "You have a next of kin who is more than willing to act as a guardian."

I pause, hoping I have some old, great aunt who wants to take me in and subsequently leave me alone.

"Who?" I ask, unable to stave my curiosity as I work back through my family tree.

"Your father."

The world spins in a similar way it did when I was in the car and my body was being thrown against the hard material of the door as glass rained down on my skin.

Except, somehow, this cuts deeper.

I'm speechless and unable to do anything other than stare at her lips that just spoke those two words out loud.

This woman, Carol from Social Services, just unlocked an opportunity for me that I'd been waiting nearly eighteen years for. She, apparently, knows who my father is when my own mother feigned for so many years that she did not.

I used to beg my mom for information, confused as to why all the people I knew at school had two parents who showed up for chorus concerts and teacher conferences, but she always deflected my questions.

Over time, I noticed the hurt in her eyes when I pried for details, so eventually, I gave up. I vowed to one day save up enough money for DNA testing or something that would help me find him on my own to satisfy my curiosity without breaking her heart in the process.

Now, it's almost cruel that the same event that caused me to lose my mother had located my father.

"My father," I repeat slowly.

Carol kindly gives me a moment to collect myself and come back to earth.

I chew on my bottom lip. "You know who he is?"

Carol and Dr. Ross respond to my question by bursting out laughing.

It hardly seems like an appropriate reaction given both of their jobs and the situation we're working through. The concept of finding something humorous seems impossible to me, and I doubt I'll ever giggle uncontrollably the way my mom and I used to do so often.

"I don't understand the joke," I tell them bitterly.

They both sober up at my words, and Carol jumps into action, rifling through my case file.

"Take a look at your birth certificate," she said simply, handing a copy of the document over to me.

I trace my mother's name—Michelle Miller—with my pointer finger.

I don't know if there are twelve steps of grief recovery, like there are in alcoholism and I can't even begin to guess what phase I'm in right now or what I'm supposed to do, but somehow, I'm comforted by the fact that her name is tied to mine in some governmental system.

I take a deep breath, and then I move my gaze over a few inches to read my father's name: Trey Carter.

"Wait," I gasp, looking back over at Dr. Ross's badge, and although I can't see it from this distance, I'm reminded of the connection.

My blood pressure surely shoots off the charts, and I can feel the pounding in my chest and ears.

"Carter, as in Carter-Churchill Medical?" I sputter.

Carol smiles tightly. "It's why you're here," she clarifies her earlier explanation. "You were airlifted from Pittsburgh as soon as he found out."

I slump back against the pillows and wait for the shock to wear off, but after a minute of silence, it doesn't.

"How do you know he's really my father?" I ask skeptically. "I mean, my mom could have written any name down or maybe..." I trail off.

It kills me that I can't simply demand answers from my mother—not that I really *demanded* anything from her in my life—but I'm unable to come up with a logical reason for her evading all of my questions.

A pit forms in my stomach, thinking the worst.

Maybe he's some sort of con man or horrible person that she wanted distance from, and now I'm trapped—legally and physically—in his care unless I buddy myself up to Carol to figure out an alternative.

Surely that's the reason she kept me hidden from him, even if she did actually put his name on the birth certificate.

"You'll see when you meet them," Carol says simply.

I blink. "Them?"

"Your father, stepmother, and brother," she explains, eyes twinkling. "They're waiting for you outside in the hall."

I cave into myself as much as my bruised body will allow me to, pressing my hand against my beating heart, unsure how much more shock my body can handle.

I survived a car accident.

And the death of my mother, which I've barely come to terms with.

And I've dealt with life on the brink of poverty and the problems that come along with it as we clawed our way out of it.

Surely if I survived all that, I can survive being thrust into a life with family I didn't know existed or even ask for.

"They're eager to officially meet you...if you're up for it."

I can tell by the smile on Carol's face that she's pushing for this, some big overjoyed event where she gets to bring a family together and have a happy ending. But there's no joy inside me to offer anyone—not one reason to smile or do anything other than get through this.

I think I can do it, though, pushing it all away with every shred of strength I have left, completely removing myself from the spiral of grief I hoped to work through in solitude and force it into dormancy.

Bury all my emotions and exist at the surface for the next nine months until I turn eighteen.

That's all I need—and then I can do anything and everything, picking up right back into the life that's waiting for me in Pennsylvania and continue on with the plans my mother and I started to form.

"What do you think?" Carol pulls me back to our conversation with a tilt of her head toward the hall.

I give myself time to take another deep breath, then slowly move my legs to hang them over the edge of the bed. Even if it's in a pair of hospital-issued socks, I feel more prepared to do this if I'm standing on my own two feet.

Dr. Ross, sensing my intention, rushes over to help me stand.

"Okay," I tell her. "I can do this."

She nods. "Yes, you can."

In the seconds it takes her to usher them inside, I make all kinds of assumptions.

He has to be some sort of a rich playboy type with a young model for a wife, who is absolutely livid by my existence and wants to turn me away before I can break up their perfect life. His son probably is some spoiled brat counting down the days until he gets a cushy job at the hospital, life handed to him on a silver platter.

All those thoughts—and the reasons I assumed my mother kept him from me—dissipate when they step into the room.

Trey smiles warmly and so does the woman beside him, as if it's a wonderful, albeit unexpected, gift that I'm suddenly appearing in their lives.

"Hello," the woman says tentatively. "I'm Heidi, and it's so wonderful to meet you."

She inches forward, offering her hand to shake.

Instinctively, I reach for it with my dominant hand, but it's in no state to be shaken all bandaged up.

She laughs when I lift my uninjured left hand, and we just kind of awkwardly hold hands for a second before I drop out of her grasp.

Heidi tucks her bright blonde hair behind her ears, beaming down at me.

"Trey, come meet your daughter," she says, reaching out a hand behind her.

Your daughter.

Those two words make me shiver, and I don't like it one bit. I remind myself that this is a temporary solution, forcing myself to remain closed, burying my emotions.

Heidi smiles at me again, shaking her head while she looks me up and down. "The resemblance is..."

"Remarkable," Trey agrees.

And the closer he gets, the more I see it.

We share honey brown eyes and jet black hair—although it's graying at his temples—and the same sharp, narrow nose.

My mom tried to talk me into getting it pierced multiple times over the summer just because she thought it would look cool, even offering to do it herself with a needle, ice cube, and apple. I declined for a number of reasons.

I doubt these two people in front of me have ever done at-home piercings, or did much of anything for themselves. I can practically smell the scent of money lingering on them.

I can't help but continue running through the comparisons between them and me.

Currently, I'm dressed in hospital-issued pajamas, but normally, I'm in bargain jeans and whatever shirt I pulled out of my drawer in the morning. They, however, are both dressed immaculately. They're casual—him with a button down, jeans, and loafers, and her with a modest summer dress and wedges—but I can tell every stitch of their clothing is expensive.

Even without the confirmation that his last name is on

the hospital, I could tell that these people have money. It's easy to see when you don't have much at all.

Despite what my birth certificate says, we might as well be from different worlds. But at least it's clear that we don't need a DNA test to confirm that I am his daughter.

"Wait for me!"

Our collective attention snaps to the doorway as a fast-moving, lanky guy about my age runs in. He's clutching one of those "IT'S A GIRL!" balloons that announce the birth of a newborn baby.

"Woah," he says, finally coming to a stop in front of me.

That one word captured the right sentiment—our looks are so similar that it's frightening, and briefly, I'm concerned that we're one of those horror stories about twins being separated at birth.

As we stare at each other, I do notice the slight differences in our facial features and shapes, but if you stuck us both in a crowd of one hundred people, we'd be picked out easily enough as being related.

He runs a hand through his disheveled hair, an I-just-woke-up-like-this perfectly messy look. "Did you separate us at birth or something?"

My throat moves like I want to admit I just had the same thought, but I don't actually open my mouth to vocalize the admission.

Trey slowly shakes his head. "I'm as shocked as you are, son."

I'm completely at a loss for what to do.

Holding everything in is simultaneously making me overwhelmed and numb, and the combination might be my new lasting temperament—another vocab word I recall.

"Benjamin," Heidi says, putting her hand on his arm. "Give the girl some breathing room."

"Right, sorry," he apologizes, making a show of tying the balloon to the edge of the hospital bed. "This is so wild."

"Wild," I repeat quietly while eyeing the absurd gesture.

"Why don't we have a seat and talk?" Carol suggests. "We have a lot to get through."

We all take seats in the little area around the television, and for as much as I wanted to stand moments ago, I'm relieved to be off my feet again.

Carol places my file on the table, along with some other things we need to talk through and sign. It's not just stuff with my custody but with my mother's death. I'll be responsible for our estate, which is a laughable word to use considering we only have a checking account, a savings account, a car that got totaled in the accident, and a small number of belongings in our apartment.

As she walks through the paperwork, my gaze is fixed on Benjamin, Heidi, and Trey.

It's almost unbelievable how these three new names I've just learned are going to be my family, for all intents and purposes, moving forward. All it took was one name on a piece of paper to make it happen.

Now, they're letting me into their life, their home, and everything else like it's normal, and all I have to do is try to get through this weird, unasked-for fantasy life in New York until June, then I can go back to reality.

FOUR

I've been out of Pennsylvania exactly twice.

Once, in celebration of my thirteenth birthday, my mom and I went on a day trip to an amusement park. I rode my first roller coaster—and absolutely loved it even though I screamed the entire time—then shared a huge serving of crispy fries slathered in melted cheese with my mom while she convinced me to spend the rest of the day on the tame rides with her, which I obliged.

And now, here, to my new life with my unexpected family.

Which has somehow landed me in the middle of New York freaking City.

It's one of the places my mother mentioned that we could visit in some distant future, imagining us spending the day wandering the city followed by a fancy dinner and a Broadway show, but we didn't even get close.

I learn quickly that the random numbers and letters that Dr. Ross rambled off to me earlier are the streets and cross streets, which is how everyone knows where anything is here. It's one of the facts I pick up from Benjamin, who hasn't stopped talking since I was discharged from the hospital.

We speed through the city in an SUV—one that looks a little too similar to the one that crashed into my mother and me—but oddly, it's not traumatic to be back in a car so quickly after the accident.

I think Benjamin's constant stream of babbling, along with the fact that I'm glued to the window, helps.

I try to take in as much as I can of the city, even though Benjamin explains to me that this area is more residential than, say, Midtown, where, apparently, most of the tourists go.

Still, there are so many storefronts and interesting people to look at that I feel like I've barely scratched the surface in the ten minutes I've been outside the hospital room.

"We're here!" Heidi announces as the car comes to a stop in front of a tall, beige brick building.

Another assumption I made crumbles at my feet. I pictured the Carters living in a mansion, some sprawling estate with horses or something, only to realize that there are no traditional houses in New York because there's no room for them.

It's ironic that I felt a little shame over the fact that my mother and I lived in a small apartment while most people I went to school with had nice, two-story homes with mortgages, separate bedrooms, and pets. But now that I'm with the richest people I've ever met, they share a building with other families just like we did back in Pennsylvania.

The concierge—named Rick, I learn—opens the door and waves me inside.

I eye the intricate red swirling pattern on his suit jacket and fidget in my pajamas and hospital socks.

Heidi apologized profusely for not having the forethought to bring a change of clothes for me with her to the hospital, but she reassured me that I could shower and change once we arrived.

I expect a grand entryway when I step through the doors, but it's actually a small square area that houses a few art pieces and armchairs along with Rick's desk and security cameras.

Trey greets him with a radiant smile, as if he's a giddy new dad, bringing his daughter back home for the first time to a freshly painted nursery.

I'm filled with apprehension—another vocabulary word—as Trey leads us around the corner to a private elevator.

We skip every single other floor until the doors open at the penthouse suite, and I gasp, finally getting the grandeur I expected.

It's a beautiful modern space, with dark floors, white walls, and silver fixtures, like something from a home decor magazine my mother used to flip through at the doctor's office.

"Welcome home," Heidi says, watching me take in my surroundings.

I step down the long hallway with a half-dozen doors to other rooms, which lead toward a terrace and an entire wall of windows that overlooks Central Park.

"Don't worry, the glass is impenetrable," Benjamin

adds. "You won't fall through or anything if you get too close. I've tested it."

Trey rolls his eyes. "I hardly call moving at full speed toward it on your electric skateboard and screaming and jumping off at the last minute 'testing it.' But something tells me that Avery is smart enough to not mimic your antics."

"Antics?" Benjamin says with a huff.

"How about you funnel that energy into giving Avery a quick tour?" Heidi suggests, looking over at me. "Or are you too tired?"

As desperate as I am to shower off and crawl into an unfamiliar bed, I do want to get my bearings. I think it will help me find a shred of normalcy in this situation and delay the inevitable big talk they're going to want to have about this entire situation.

In the hospital, Carol kept us on track talking about logistics and paperwork, but I have a suspicion they'll eventually want to dive into emotions and whatnot, which I'd love to avoid entirely in favor of sleeping for one thousand years.

"A tour sounds good," I say.

"Cool," Benjamin returns with a nod.

"And I've asked our housekeeper to set aside a few things of mine until we can get you your own clothes and everything else you need."

"Okay," I say numbly. "And thank you."

Trey wraps an arm around Heidi and offers me another smile. "We're glad you're here, Avery. I mean it."

"This is your home now," Heidi adds, causing my chest

to tighten. "You should feel comfortable here, but don't hesitate to let us know if you need anything at all."

I swallow and cross my arms, physically trying to hold myself together as they retreat into what Benjamin quickly confirms is their bedroom.

He then offers me an arm, a gesture I stare at for at least four blinks until he nudges the air beside me, encouraging me to slip my hand through it.

I decide to relent, even though he drags me around the space a little roughly for how battered I feel.

I think this gesture feels more formal to him, which is why he has adopted a horrifically bad British accent as he explains the layout to me.

There's a gym, several bathrooms, a few bedrooms, an office, an oversized kitchen, and a formal dining room. The terrace I eyed earlier has some real live grass growing in the center of it, which is just as impressive as it is ridiculous.

I'm silent as I take it all in, but Benjamin has no problem filling the void, pointing out various nicks on the walls that he created mistakenly and where art pieces used to be before they got broken and subsequently moved elsewhere.

Finally, after a quick peek into his dark blue bedroom, with a massive television and every gaming system imaginable, he opens the door next to it.

"This is your room," he says proudly. "It's kind of plain and blah right now, but I bet my mom will help you pick out new stuff if you want."

It's a clean, white room with a queen canopy bed, oversized dresser, vanity, walk-in closet, and attached bathroom.

If I could whistle, I'd do it now.

I'm having a hard time wrapping my head around the fact that this is supposed to be my personal space because I definitely do not belong here.

I rub my eyes, wondering if my concussion has actually just caused my brain to create some sort of alternate reality for myself, but when I open them again, the scenery hasn't changed.

"Martha's the best," Benjamin says, pulling my attention over to the nightstand.

There's a wicker basket stuffed with chocolate, candles, and a small teddy bear holding a "Welcome home, Avery!" note between its two paws.

"Who's Martha?" I ask him.

"Our housekeeper slash nanny slash cook slash Wonder Woman," he gushes. "She originally started working here when I was a kid to babysit while my parents were busy with work. Even though, obviously, I don't need a nanny anymore, she still puts up with us."

"Oh," I breathe.

That one sentence alone shows how drastically different our upbringings were.

Benjamin chuckles. "I'm pretty sure she and Rick, the guy from downstairs, are hooking up, but Caleb and Ethan say I'm just projecting my own unrequited love onto other people."

I push against the pull of exhaustion to focus on his words. "Caleb and Ethan?"

"My best friends," he explains. "We've known each other forever. They live downstairs, so I'm sure you'll meet them soon. I mean, they practically live up here, anyway."

I open the wide set of drawers, breathing a sigh of relief that there are actually clean and comfortable clothes waiting for me after I shower.

I rifle through it until my hands land on a matching sweatshirt and sweatpants that feel soft. I know it's still warm for September, but there's something comforting about being all wrapped up, and I need it right now.

Benjamin rolls onto the bed and lies back, lazily chewing on a piece of chocolate from the set Martha left for me.

I'm trying to figure out a polite way to get him to leave so I can shower, but Benjamin doesn't pick up on my eagerness to wash the hospital—and everything else—off me.

"I always considered them to be like my brothers, because you know it gets kind of lonely being an only child, but now I have a sister," he continues. "They're going to be so jealous."

I snort at that. "Jealous? Of me or of you?"

He considers it while he unwraps another little chocolate truffle. "Both, I think. Blood relation to me? Awesome. A little sister to chill with? Even better."

That is really sweet of him to say, and it slightly dampens my annoyance of not being left alone.

"Little sister?" I clarify, clutching the clothes to my chest. "When's your birthday?"

"June third," he says.

"I'm June first."

He sits up, excitement clear in his eyes. "Who cares about the dates? We can have a joint birthday party! Like how Caleb and Ethan used to before we all decided birthday parties were kind of lame." Benjamin pauses and gives me an earnest look. "But this, I can assure you, will not be lame."

Although it would be easy to dash that dream, I don't do it.

He doesn't have to know right now that I plan on leaving the very minute I turn eighteen. It's probably better that I go along with whatever the Carters want from me right now, so I keep it to myself.

"I'm going to go get cleaned up," I say, making my way to the bathroom.

"Hey, Avery?"

I stop in the doorway. "Hey, Benjamin?"

"Just promise me you won't date them," he says with a frown.

I blink. "Excuse me?"

"It's just...they're my best friends, and you're my sister...and yeah."

I'm unable to comprehend this demand—not just because he asked me to not have romantic feelings for people I've never met but because he thinks with all the trauma I've endured, I would even have the mental capacity to consider dating someone right now.

"Okay," I agree softly.

He seems satisfied with that enough to pull out his phone. "Good," he says. "I'm going to start researching ideas for our party."

I shake off our conversation and fill my brain with the next immediate tasks—stripping my clothes, ripping off my bandages, turning on the water, and washing slowly and carefully.

Dr. Ross gave me strict instructions to be gentle with

my wounds, so I take my time with each movement. The relief of the warm water on my scalp is incredible, and I do an adequate job of washing my hair one-handed.

As the steam billows around me, I test myself.

I give my inner conscious permission to break down completely under the faucet, unleashing the magnitude of every single emotion I've buried since waking up at the hospital.

But now that I have the solitude to do so, I actually don't feel the need to.

Oddly, I'm at peace, just focusing on what I need to do to take care of myself.

There are plenty of things circling in the event of my mother's death—more paperwork, insurance company stuff, an obituary—but in my "fragile state," as Carol put it, Trey insisted on taking care of these matters for me. I can't decide if I hate myself for allowing him to do it.

I suppose we have an instant line of trust, being genetically connected, but it's also not like I have another option. I don't want to rely on them for emotional, financial, or any other support, but I'm stuck, bound by the State of New York.

After I step out of the shower, I towel dry my hair and slip on Heidi's borrowed clothes before I patch myself back up. Most of the cuts from the shattered glass already have a protective scab over them, but I still place bandages on them before I tape the fingers on my right hand.

I pointedly avoid looking at my face in the mirror, choosing instead to give myself over to emptiness and exhaustion instead of staring at the mark across my cheek.

I crack open the door, and thankfully, Benjamin and his chocolate wrappers are nowhere to be found.

The bottle of pain pills from Dr. Ross sits on my nightstand with a glass of water, along with a note from Heidi.

Avery, I hope you're settling in okay. We're all thinking of you and are here if you need us for anything. -Heidi

Even though it's the middle of the afternoon, I tuck myself into my gigantic, comfortable bed and fall into a deep sleep.

FIVE

I wake up in unfamiliarity but not discomfort.

While stretching out the tightness in my limbs, I roll over to see it's just past six in the morning, which means I slept for nearly sixteen hours.

I've never been one of those people who needs a lot of sleep, but my mother always did—she was grouchy and in need of coffee if she got anything less than eight, which happened more often than not.

My stomach growls, reawakened right along with the rest of me, but the chocolate at my bedside doesn't appeal to me at this hour.

During yesterday's tour, my jaw dropped open when Benjamin showed their walk-in pantry to me—it's almost like a little grocery store in a house, with neat rows of brand-name food and glass jars containing various flours and pastas.

I pop a round of pain pills and drain the glass of water, then I stand up from my bed on shaky legs and slowly make my way toward the kitchen. I feel a little weird about helping myself to food, even though I think they would encourage it.

"Avery?"

I nearly jump out of my skin at the sound of my name.

"Sorry, dear, I didn't mean to scare you." A gray-haired woman waves me in the kitchen. "I'm Martha."

"Nice to meet you," I say politely. "And thank you for the chocolates."

"Heidi told me last night that Benjamin helped himself," she says in an annoyed tone. "So if you'll tell me your favorites, I'll restock it."

"Oh, that's okay," I tell her.

She raises her eyebrows, like I don't have a choice in the matter, before she takes a deep breath and says, "Well, how about some coffee?"

I shake my head. "No. Thank you, though."

"You won't get far with being shy in this city, Avery." Her words are sharp, but her eyes are kind. "You need to be direct with what you want, especially in this house. Got it?"

"Got it," I say.

"Now, can I get you a coffee?"

"I'm not much for caffeine," I admit, not wanting to decline her once again. "But if you have tea, I'll take it."

She smiles in approval and opens a cabinet stuffed with boxes of various brands and flavors. "What's your poison?"

"The Mint Medley sounds good."

"Trey's favorite," she says casually while retrieving the box. "Go have a seat in the dining room and let me finish up here. I'll bring it in along with a plate of breakfast for you when it's ready."

Unlike Benjamin, I can pick up when I'm being dismissed. "Thank you."

I take a seat at the massive dining table, running my fingers across the smooth wooden surface. It's polished and pristine, the exact opposite of what I left behind back home in Pennsylvania.

Recalling that fact would have felt like a stabbing pain yesterday, but at the moment, it's brought up with no emotion, like I'm just recalling an endless number of facts from my mind.

At the head of the table, there are a few national newspapers stacked neatly along with a pen.

I'm itching to do the crossword puzzle, something I indulged in every single Sunday.

Usually, my mom had the early shift, doing prep work before the restaurant opened, and I'd sit in the car trying to get as many boxes filled in until my hostess duties started at eleven o'clock.

"You're up early," Trey says, entering the dining room with two cups in his hands.

He drops a mug in front of me, which I accept gratefully, before he sinks into his spot.

"And you're feeling well?"

The truth is, I'm feeling absolutely nothing, and it's on purpose.

"I'm okay," is what I end up saying.

We stare at each other momentarily in awkward silence.

It's understandable, given our nonexistent history, but it doesn't make it any easier to sit through.

This man went from being a complete stranger to a father to me overnight. Now, he's invested, financially and emotionally, in my well-being.

We share genetics and features, but we don't really know anything about each other. I'm not sure how deep I want to go with establishing this relationship, but this stiffness between us is so uncomfortable, I have to try to fill it.

"Do you do the crossword?" I ask.

"I try to, but usually Ethan finishes it," he admits, flipping open *The New York Times* to the right place.

He's about to dismiss the topic altogether, but he sees the way I'm looking at it longingly.

"How about you start, and we can try to fill in the blanks together?"

"Okay," I say, reaching for the pen, grateful that the tape on my fingers doesn't throw off my writing too much.

With my attention taken up by figuring out the little clues while Trey works through emails on his phone, the quiet morning is actually tolerable.

Martha steps in and drops full plates for us of warm, buttery waffles, crispy turkey bacon, scrambled eggs, and fruit slices.

I sip my tea and pick at my fruit, already a third of the way through the puzzle by the time Heidi comes in the room.

"Good morning!" She's exceptionally chipper and already dressed for the day. "Sleep well, Avery?"

"Yes, thank you."

Trey and Heidi chatter away about some hospital charity event that I think Heidi is responsible for planning, giving me plenty of time to work on a few more clues. I luck out that "apex," one of my vocabulary words, is in a pivotal spot.

Martha brings in a plate for Heidi and adds more hot water to our cups.

"Okay, Avery, it's been long enough," Trey says.

His words startle me, and a pit forms in my stomach at the attention.

I was just getting comfortable enough to sit here undisturbed, and I'm not mentally prepared to sort through all the history and emotion that they want to unpack.

"What are you stuck on?" Trey asks, nodding to the paper.

I stop the relieved sigh from escaping my mouth. "Oh, uh, capital of Greece?"

"Athens," Heidi answers excitedly before turning to me. "We were just there in the spring, celebrating fifteen years of marriage, and twenty years together."

I quickly do the math of those numbers in my head.

If that's the timeline of their relationship, I'm baffled by the fact that she's okay with my being here. So far, she's embraced me completely—although not literally; I didn't let anyone get that close and personal to me yesterday—but I'm on edge still.

I expect at some point she'll turn on me, the reminder that Trey likely cheated on her when they were younger.

Trey clears his throat. "Next?"

"Japanese mushroom. Eight letters. Third letter is an I."

"Shiitake," he says easily.

"Which we discovered my Aunt Lisa was allergic to when she bit into an appetizer at my thirtieth surprise party," Heidi says. "Truly, I forgot about it while planning the menu."

"There's usually a story for every clue," Trey explains to me. "It's why it usually takes us all breakfast until the boys show up in time for Ethan to finish it."

"You planned your own party?" I ask, wondering if this was why Benjamin was so eager to work out the details for ours last night.

"Of course," Heidi says. "If I let Trey do it all, it would have been a disaster, so I planned it exactly the way I wanted it to go, and I got to watch all of our friends squirm to not spoil anything for weeks leading up to it and act all surprised on the actual day." She laughs at her own recollection. "So it was kind of an added bonus to it."

I chew on my lip. "Sounds like it."

Heidi and Trey reminisce about the party and some memories with their friends, and we fill in a few more answers on the puzzle.

It's like one of those scenes in a television show with a full, beautiful breakfast, only instead of dashing off and leaving a full glass of orange juice behind, we enjoy it together.

I take a massive bite of a blueberry waffle that's so fluffy and delicious, if I had any tears left, I would certainly weep.

"So, Avery," Heidi says, addressing me directly. "Do you think you're up for a round of shopping today?"

Her tone is one of excitement, like I should be itching to go explore the city and watch her swipe her credit card, but the idea makes me uncomfortable.

Rationally, I know I'm going to depend on their money for food and housing, but to go spend money as an excuse to spend time together seems superfluous—another vocabulary word.

"I don't mind borrowing your clothes until we can get the stuff from—"

"Nonsense," she insists, waving her hand in the air. "We'll need to get your uniforms tailored, and as wonderful as you look in my clothing, I'm sure you'd like some stuff for yourself."

"Uniforms?"

Despite my dedication to academia, the actual school I've attended hasn't mattered to me. Out of all the topics we addressed yesterday with Carol, I didn't even think to ask about school. I've been to so many different ones over the years that as long as my credits transferred and I could keep up, I was fine.

"I know," she sighs. "It's a little antiquated, but they're not that bad. Especially since we'll get you a new school bag and whatever other items you want to accessorize it with."

"Accessorize," I repeat, thinking of my beat-up black JanSport that's probably still on the hook in the apartment in Pennsylvania.

She brushes right past it. "And after the tailor's, we can swing by Bloomingdale's to get you some casual clothes and the other essentials."

Benjamin appears in the doorway. "Can I come?"

"You want to go shopping?" Trey asks as Benjamin drops into the seat beside me.

"I want to go to Bloomingdale's," he clarifies.

"Which means he wants to go to Magnolia Bakery," Heidi explains to me. "It's a fairly famous spot right inside the entrance of the store. I think it was mentioned in *Sex and the City* and *The Devil Wears Prada* if you've seen either of those."

And here I thought our Target at home was cool for having a Starbucks in it.

"They have the best banana pudding," Benjamin gushes. "And magic cookie bars...and brownies...and cupcakes."

I swallow another bite of Martha's home cooking. "So the best of everything?"

"Pretty much," he says, swiping a piece of bacon from my plate.

"Benjamin, manners," Trey admonishes him.

"Yeah, manners, Benjamin," a mocking, gravelly tone says.

My gaze snaps up to the voice, and I have to choke down my bite with effort as I take in the two newcomers.

"Avery!" Benjamin says excitedly. "These are my best friends. This is Caleb and that's Ethan. And guys, this is my little sister, Avery."

It takes me a fraction of a second to understand exactly what was behind Benjamin's random and completely inappropriate no-dating rule.

Holy hell, these two are gorgeous.

Although they're twins, they seem to have two completely different styles and demeanors.

At first glance, Caleb embodies the prep school persona, with his light brown hair cut short and trendy glasses that likely don't have a prescription in the lenses. Ethan's got an edgier vibe about him, with his dark hair hitting just below his shoulders and his arms crossed on his chest.

And they've both got killer blue eyes that are fixed on the ugly gash across my face.

Suddenly, the idea of eating seems repulsive, so I slide my plate out of the way and refocus on the puzzle, rolling the pen between my thumb and index finger.

"Athletic challenge with five events," I say to Trey, acting as if their gawking didn't bother me one bit. "Ten letters. Second letter is E."

"Pentathlon," Ethan says immediately, taking the seat across from mine.

Heidi laughs, waving to Martha in gratitude as she drops off plates for the boys. "I don't have a story for that."

I swallow. "James Bond's vehicle of choice. Eleven letters. Fourth letter is O. Last letter is N."

"Aston Martin," Trey answers, and before Heidi can speak, he adds, "Benjamin once had a James Bond–themed birthday party."

Benjamin frowns. "It wasn't one of my better ideas. But, hey, little sis and I are going to have a joint birthday party this year, since ours are so close."

"Avery is two days older than you, Benjamin," Heidi clarifies.

"And I'm exactly eight minutes older than Ethan," Caleb tells me.

Ethan rolls his eyes. "Yeah, and it's not like you forever hold that over me or anything."

I can barely keep up as they all banter and joke around with one another.

There are layers of history I recognize here, built up from years of friendship, camaraderie, and meals like this one.

I never found anything like this dynamic aside from my mother, but surely at least someone cared about me enough back home to wonder where I went.

"Heidi," I mumble before I can think better of it. "Did the hospital retrieve my purse or anything else from the crash?"

"Not yet," she answers evenly. "Don't worry about money, Avery, we'll take care of everything today."

"I was hoping to get my phone back," I blurt. "See if anyone called me about…" I trail off, not quite ready to finish that sentence aloud.

"We'll take care of it this week," Trey promises. "There's still some paperwork, and I think everything's being held at the police station with your mother—"

He abruptly stops, and so does the conversation around the table.

Well, at least it's comforting to know that everyone is up to speed on my recent trauma, which should spare me from some awkward conversations.

"So, is everyone coming shopping?" Benjamin asks before stealing another piece of bacon from my plate. "And to Magnolia?"

"If you want to," Heidi offers.

"Subject Change Five!" Caleb holds up his hand.

My gaze snaps to him, and Benjamin starts to explain to me how in the show *Scrubs*, one of the characters wants to be known as "The High Five Guy," so at random moments during the episodes, he shows up offering a "Five" with whatever point applies to the dialogue.

I, being the medical show nerd that I am, already know this, so I lean across the table. "Acknowledgment Five," I say, earning a genuine laugh from Caleb, along with a quick slap of our palms.

"A Sacred Heart fan," Caleb says appreciatively.

It's oddly reassuring that out of all the newness and assurances made in the past twenty-four hours, I find the most comfort in bonding over something so silly.

Heidi and Trey look surprised at the motion, but Ethan groans.

"Ethan doesn't appreciate the finer reruns of life," Caleb tells me.

"I did...once, but then it turned into getting an overanalyzed take on every patient's supposed illness, and it became too much to sit with a walking medical encyclopedia," Ethan explains, tilting his head toward his brother.

"Caleb might know more about the medical industry than any of us at this point," Trey explains, "and I own a damn hospital."

"Which means that someday, you'll have no choice but to hire me," Caleb says.

"Let's not get ahead of ourselves, Dr. Navarro," Trey retorts. "First, let's focus on graduating high school."

I watch them all fall back into easy and light conversation until we all scatter to get ready for the day ahead.

SIX

A few days later, the four of us walk to school as a group.

We navigate around commuters and people coming to and from workout classes. The sounds of the city—sirens in the distance, cars whipping by, random yelling—are sporadic and jarring, along with the smells of coffee, hot pastries, and trash.

It's sensory overload.

And it makes me feel like I've reached another plane of existence.

This is a ridiculous thought given my recent brush with death, but the act of trying to get from place to place requires so much attention that every sense is heightened.

But at least all this is distracting me from my nervousness over starting a new school.

I should be used to starting over by now, but public schools in Pennsylvania all blend together, and I don't know how different they'll be from a private school in Manhattan.

I'm trying to take in the storefronts and streets while being physically pulled along by Benjamin, with Caleb and Ethan trailing right behind me.

Dr. Ross warned me not to push myself too hard these first few weeks, and I'm practically jogging along at this point.

"Is he always like this?" I ask the twins, a little exasperated.

"It depends if you're referring to his overeagerness for punctuality or his excitement at seeing Brooke Collins before the first period," Ethan says.

"Who is Brooke Collins?" I ask.

Benjamin laughs loudly but doesn't turn. "Who is Brooke Collins?" he repeats, as if it's the dumbest question I could have asked.

It goes unanswered even as we head up the stairs and inside the lobby.

At my last school, you were lucky to get a plate of grease before the day started, but here, there's a sleek coffee stand with a case full of French pastries.

I expect Benjamin to beeline for the sweets, which I now know he eats by the armful, but he leads us over to one of the vacant seating areas near the main office.

"I'm all set on enrollment stuff," I remind him. "I've already got my schedule and whatnot."

A packet of information containing my schedule and course material arrived around the same time my freshly altered uniforms got delivered. I'd tried everything on and stared at my schedule before I went to bed, wanting to be prepared.

"This isn't for your benefit," Caleb explains, sinking into the seat beside me. "It's for his."

He pushes up the trendy glasses on his nose, and I follow the line of his gaze, landing on a tall girl with box braids, dyed a really cool shade of red, who smiles at the barista.

"She only drinks iced coffee," Benjamin says, watching the exchange. "Even in the winter."

I wrinkle my nose. "This is kind of..."

"Borderline stalker?" Ethan offers.

"I take great offense to that," Benjamin says.

Caleb levels with him. "You spent an hour last Thursday looking at paint swatches to find a name for just the right shade of her hair."

"It was between Read Red and Positive Red," Ethan explains for my benefit.

I've allowed myself to settle in, slightly, to this new life with the Carters, but I have to keep reminding myself not to get too emotionally invested.

This is a temporary solution.

But even that notion doesn't stave my curiosity.

"Does she not...like you or something?" I ask tentatively.

Caleb and Ethan both burst out laughing, and Benjamin looks sheepish.

"What's so funny?" I glance up in time to see the new addition, a tiny brunette, slide onto Caleb's lap. "And who's this?"

She eyes me and the gash on my face while her brow shoots up in a perfectly done arch, waiting for someone to explain my presence.

"This is Avery," Caleb says, lazily putting an arm around her waist. "Avery, this is Sophia."

I'm compelled to avert my eyes from their blatant intimacy, and instinctively, I shift to the other side of the chair.

"You're new?" Sophia asks me directly.

"I'm Benjamin's sister."

It's the first time I've said those words out loud, and it's an action that causes him to turn away from watching Brooke and offer me a ridiculously toothy smile.

She laughs. "Since when?"

"We just found out about each other," I say, not wanting to offer too many details about my backstory.

Sophia doesn't drop it. "And now, suddenly, you go to school with us?"

It's obvious, given that we're both wearing the same uniforms that seem straight out of *Gossip Girl*, but I give her the benefit of the doubt.

"Yeah, I kind of live here now."

"Hmm," is all she offers, still sizing me up.

I don't need her to think I'm the enemy or competition when I'm just trying to get through this school year—or at least to start this first day.

I grab my schedule out of my bag, clutching both things like they're a lifeline to use as my excuse to get out of this, and stand quickly.

"Well, see you guys later," I say before I head for the stairs.

"Hey, Avery, wait up," Ethan calls. "Do you know where you're going?"

"English."

"With Mayberry?"

I nod. "Yeah."

He smooths his long hair back. "Cool, me too. I'll walk with you."

As we make our way up the stairs, he gives me the basic rundown of the school, which is four stories high. Instead of organizing by grade, it's by wings of subjects, and I, apparently, have lucked out on a schedule that doesn't send me running up and down all the flights of stairs between each period.

When we arrive at the correct classroom, Ms. Mayberry welcomes me to the school and encourages me to sit anywhere in the circle of seats.

Ethan tilts his head to the vacant spot beside him.

"This is a discussion-heavy class," Ethan explains as I settle in. "She says that arranging the desks like this fosters openness and collaboration."

"Does it?" I ask. "Foster anything?"

Ethan shrugs. "I really think it's so she can make sure all of us are awake or not just playing around on our phones."

The other students arrive, and every single one of them stares at me with casual interest.

I try my best to be okay with it, but eventually, I fidget under the scrutiny.

It's not that I have a problem with the scar, which still needs time to heal, but it's the fact that it's something I can't control, something that makes me stand out and calls attention without my permission. Every time I catch a lingering gaze, it's like a zap in the back of my subconscious as a reminder how I got it and what happened.

I untuck my hair from my ears, trying to use it as a

shield as I sink back in my chair, a motion that doesn't go unnoticed by Ethan, who offers me a tight smile.

After the bell rings, I'm given a quick introduction by Ms. Mayberry, satisfying everyone's curiosity for the time being before she gives us all instructions for a writing exercise.

Ethan and I partner up, knocking out a list of top ten character traits in any worthwhile protagonist, which apparently is going to cue us up for the next unit.

The other students are taking their time with the assignment, arguing a little over their lists.

"It's not so bad here," he whispers to me. "They're just staring because you're new."

"Sure," I say, looking around the room.

Minus the uniforms, it's just like any other high school classroom setting I've been in.

"I think I can survive here for now."

"For now?"

"I turn eighteen in June," I say, the words slipping out of my mouth before I give it a second thought.

"And then what?" he asks curiously. "You turn into a pumpkin and run back to Pennsylvania?"

I frown. "Hopefully not the pumpkin part."

He taps his pen against his desk, then cautiously looks at me again. "You're really planning on leaving?"

"I mean, once I'm legal, the Carters aren't obligated to shelter, clothe, and feed me, so...yes."

"You think that they're the kind of people who are just sitting here and counting down the days until they can get rid of you?" Ethan says, shaking his head in disbelief.

I don't think that, but I don't really know what to expect from them.

"I don't know yet," I admit. "I only found out I had a father a few days ago, so I think it's going to take some time to process it all."

His forehead scrunches up, as if he's trying to find the right words to placate me, but the teacher calls for our attention again.

"Well, I guess we'll see," he says to me before we're caught up in the rest of class.

I don't know if he's in the position to promise that, but I tuck his words into a spot at the forefront of my mind.

For the next few classes, I'm on my own.

I find my way around easily enough, but I feel awkward stepping in each new classroom, like I'm intruding on something I'm not supposed to be involved in. In fact, that pretty much sums up how I've felt since I got here.

As uncomfortable as I felt during the shopping and lunch outing last weekend, I'm almost glad that there were so many of us wandering around the stores and huddled around a table. It took the pressure off me to speak much at all—then again, Benjamin has no problem filling gaps in any conversation.

But the dynamics of human interactions are complicated.

I suppose it just gets easier with time, and I'm hopeful as the day continues on because faces become familiar and I'm stared at a little less.

I actually manage to let myself get a little excited as I walk to the science wing for my next class, anatomy. I've always excelled at the sciences and loved learning about the biology and chemistry of what makes us capable of existing.

Now, I get to take a course that allows me to further my knowledge. Of course, I've watched many dissection and surgery videos on the internet, along with every fictional and documentary-style medical show in existence, but this will help.

I walk in as the bell rings, immediately catching Caleb's eye at the back of the room.

He smiles and mouths "Air Five!" before Sophia rolls her eyes and makes him drop his hand.

Once I've checked in with the teacher, I see that the only seat unclaimed is next to the same girl who is the object of Benjamin's affection.

She smiles and waves me over. "Hey, you're new, right? I'm Brooke."

"Avery," I say, sitting beside her. "And yeah, I just moved here."

Up close, I get a better look at her, and on the surface, I can understand Benjamin's infatuation—although I definitely don't agree with his approach.

There's something about her smile and vibe that puts me immediately at ease.

"From where?"

"Pennsylvania."

"Never been," she says, pulling out her textbook, notebook, and laptop.

I do the same, and a *Good luck on your first day!* note from Heidi falls out. I stuff it back into the bag she insisted I needed to have, along with the new suite of electronics.

"But I hear Philly's fun," Brooke adds.

"I'm from the other side of the state, unfortunately so—"

The teacher clears his throat at the front of the class. "Most of you seem to have forgotten today is the first day of our dissection. Clear your tables, and prepare the kits."

"I totally forgot," Brooke says.

I don't miss the way her eyes go wide.

If I remember the syllabus correctly, I don't think we were due to dissect anything until the end of the year at my old school, and I'm ecstatic to get hands-on experience my very first day.

Brooke and I make quick work of getting set up, and the teacher slides the tray with the frog we're meant to dissect on our table.

As I'm organizing our set of tools, she says, "Look, I'm not one to sit back and let someone else do all the work but..."

"I got this," I tell her, gingerly gripping the scalpel between my uninjured fingers.

Brooke and I end up making a pretty good team. I tackle the actual slicing while she takes notes and points out what exactly we should look for in the dissection.

I can't help but think about how interesting bodies are, just a mix of muscles and chemicals.

I wonder if the surgeon who removed my appendix years ago shared my enthusiasm for this project when she was in high school. It's an enormous leap—pun intended—but everyone has to start somewhere.

When the teacher announces we have five minutes until the bell rings, I frown, while Brooke lets out a breath of relief.

"Not that I have much of an appetite at the moment, but I was wondering if you have lunch plans?" Brooke says to me once we've finished our lesson and cleaned up.

"I don't think so," I say hesitantly.

"She does," Caleb jumps in, catching up to us with Sophia still glued by his side. "But you're welcome to join us for Meatless Monday in the dining hall."

"You're a vegetarian?" I ask, recalling that he watched Benjamin eat many pieces of bacon at the Carters' place.

He shrugs. "I am for tofu tacos."

"That sounds pretty good," Brooke agrees. "Especially after today's class...I think I'm good on not eating meat for a while."

Sophia scoffs. "Have you been eating a lot of frogs lately?"

I trail behind the three of them as we make our way downstairs.

It's not like one of those typical high school cafeterias with long tables that fold up and wheel away—it feels like a restaurant with different sizes of tables and seating options.

We're still on the topic of today's anatomy class when Benjamin and Ethan finally join us at the table.

"And like I was telling her, I just don't think she understands the allegory I created with all the *GoldenEye* references. She didn't even comment on my very hilarious joke about ranking who was the best actor to play James Bond."

Ethan sighs audibly. "You lectured our teacher, who has a PhD in history, about a game you play on a console that's older than you are while trying to argue your grade on a paper that was supposed to be about the Vietnam War? And you can't see why she doesn't agree?"

As they continue, Brooke's brows furrow, trying to solve the puzzle that's in her mind as she takes in the resemblance between Benjamin and me.

"Brother," I say by way of explanation.

She blinks. *"You* are related to *him?"*

I can't decide if I want to take offense to that statement, but the clanging of silverware captures my attention.

Benjamin sputters and picks up his cutlery, trying to avoid all eye contact with Brooke.

He's suddenly...shy?

The Benjamin who brought a balloon to meet his new sister and made himself at home on her bed suddenly is retreating into himself so much, it's almost painful to watch.

We've barely established our relationship as siblings, and as much as I don't want to get overly involved, I already feel compelled to protect and help him—even if it's something as trivial as having a crush on someone.

"Yes," I say a little coldly. "Is there something about it that surprises you?"

My tone is challenging, and after days of a monotone lifelessness, I don't hate the sound of it.

Brooke grimaces, realizing the way her question came across. "I just meant that you two seem so different in personality," she says, scrambling to step back on her words.

"Because Avery probably has better grades than him on the first day?" Ethan adds. "And he doesn't even realize he has his sweater on backward?"

Brooke looks at me for validation, and I sigh as Benjamin's face flushes red when he realizes he does, in fact, have his sweater on backward.

Thankfully, Ethan changes the subject. "How's your first day going so far?"

"Okay, I think. At least, I've figured out where all my classes are and didn't have to do the whole 'introduce yourself in front of everyone' thing."

"Even then, you're all anyone can talk about," Sophia says, not totally unkindly. "Everyone keeps asking about where that—" She gestures to the cut along my face. "—is from."

"Car accident," Benjamin says, finally finding his voice to spare me from having to say those words.

"That's what I told them," she shoots back. "But the stories kept getting wilder, and then I just couldn't let it go on like that."

"Like what?" I ask her.

"*Boring*. Car accident, getting jumped on the subway, a trip and fall, blah, blah, blah. Little to no creativity. So I told everyone in third period that you got in a knife fight." She pauses. "And won, obviously."

"A knife fight," I repeat.

"You should see the other guy," she says with a wink.

I can't decide if Sophia wants me dead or wants to be my best friend.

"It's kind of believable, I mean, you should have seen her with a scalpel," Caleb jumps in. "It's frightening."

The entire table comes together, coming up with more brave and ridiculous scenarios, like how I saved a newborn baby from getting run over by a cab.

"Got a lot of homework to do tonight?" Ethan asks, attempting to pull us into our own little side conversation.

My gut reaction is that I haven't checked the schedule yet to see if I'm on the shift for tonight...only to remember that isn't my life anymore and my schedule is completely open. I no longer have to rush from school to the restaurant, fitting in homework on my break and in the time between showering and sleeping.

"Yeah," I say.

I'm slowly accumulating a mountain of makeup work that will need to be tackled as soon as possible if I have any shot at maintaining my GPA and earning as many scholarships as I can.

"Do you guys always hang out after school?" I ask him.

"Usually," Ethan says between bites of chips.

"Is homework done during this time, or is it exclusively for messing around?"

He laughs. "Usually the latter, but I'm more than happy to have someone around who actually cares about school. Despite what Ben argues, I don't think playing old N64 games will help you get straight A's."

"Hey," my brother cuts in, only to once again have his attention stolen by Brooke, who stands up and gathers her trash.

He watches her cross the dining hall, stopping to talk to another group of people at a table before she throws away her leftovers.

"What do you mean by that?" Sophia snaps at Caleb.

I don't know what he said to warrant such a reaction, but I'm guessing they're having some sort of misunderstanding if I'm reading their body language correctly.

Caleb takes off his glasses so he can pinch the bridge of his nose between his thumb and pointer finger. "Not what you think, Soph."

They argue in loud tones, and I refocus on Ethan, trying to give them some privacy in this very public setting.

"Here we go again," Ethan says under his breath. "It's the inevitable weekly fight before the breakup."

"Want to take a bet on how long this one lasts?" Benjamin asks him.

"You still owe me one hundred bucks from the last one."

"And I'm pretty sure you still owe me two hundred from the time before that."

Ethan chuckles, and Benjamin joins him, increasing the sound dramatically to act like he has been having the time of his life when Brooke comes back to grab her bag.

"Coming, Soph?" she asks.

Sophia glares at Caleb before they both leave, even though the bell hasn't rung yet.

As soon as they're out of earshot, Benjamin says, "So, do you guys think Brooke is interested in me?"

The twins answer him with a collective groan.

SEVEN

I spend the rest of my first week trying to stay afloat.

Even though it's only a few days, it feels like I have more to do than I did in the first month at my old school.

Outside of the piling assignments to catch up on, I hold onto my distance as best I can. I try to keep all the conversations surface-level, but the more time I spend in the whirlwind that is Benjamin, the boldness that is Caleb, and the wittiness that is Ethan, I can't help but try to figure out my own place in their world.

And I'm not sure if it's healthy for me to continue doing so.

We walk to school together, see one another in some classes, eat lunch together. After school, Ethan and I do homework together while Caleb and Benjamin seem to do anything but be productive. Occasionally, they drag Ethan into refereeing a wrestling match or playing a game, but I'm content to watch and attempt to get caught up.

By the time Friday night rolls around, I've barely gotten

enough of a handle on the coursework to see how behind I am.

It's not really a surprise the curriculum from my large, public high school in Pennsylvania didn't exactly mesh up with this elite private school in New York.

Benjamin tries his best to get me to go out with him, Ethan, and Caleb, but I'm ready for a quiet night alone with my books and new laptop, which I can barely figure out how to work.

I quickly plow through my anatomy assignments, but my brain hits a wall two pages in on my history paper. I don't really find the subject of the American economy fascinating, so I've resorted to using the thesaurus to help me pad the word count. Brevity—another vocabulary word—has never been more of my specialty until recently.

Heidi knocks on my door as she opens it. "Avery? You stayed in?"

She eyes my position on the floor, with my computer balancing on my knees and the contents of my bag spilled out beside me.

I'm embarrassed that she sees how messy I'm being, and I hope she doesn't take it as a sign of disrespect.

"Sorry, I'll clean this up."

"Don't worry about it," she says. "I didn't come in here to monitor the organization of your bedroom."

I push the books into a neat pile anyway, lining up all the spines and pushing the papers into organized chaos.

Heidi leans on the doorframe. "You didn't want to go out with the boys?"

"I have a lot to catch up on," I say, gesturing to everything around me. "But thanks for stopping in."

I try to dismiss her, but just like when I try to with Benjamin, she doesn't pick up on it—or chooses not to.

"Come on, Avery," she says, standing up straight in a show of authority. "It's time for a dessert break."

"Oh no, that's—"

"If you're insisting on staying locked in your bedroom when you're at the prime of your teenage years, you might as well do it hopped up on sugar."

She's out the door before I can disagree.

If I wasn't just a little bit annoyed by the act, I'd be impressed. Even then, I sigh, resigning to follow the flash of her blonde hair as she rounds the corner to the kitchen.

"How do you feel about ice cream?" Heidi asks.

"Pretty good about it."

She smiles, then opens the expansive slide-out drawer.

I didn't even know there were all sorts of options for the arrangement of a refrigerator and freezer until I walked into this kitchen for the first time.

I make myself useful, grabbing us each a spoon from the drawer, then I perch up on one of the fancy velvet barstools and watch Heidi move around, elbows deep in the freezer.

She pulls out carton after carton of Ben & Jerry's, waiting until I signal which one I want.

My mouth waters when my eyes land on Chunky Monkey. It's been too long since I've had that perfect combination of ice cream, walnuts, bananas, and chocolate. My mother and I usually stuck to store-brand ice cream cartons and whatever desserts we could wrangle from the restaurant.

I open the lid and dive right in, earning soft laughter

from Heidi, who just reached for bowls off the open shelving.

"Oh," I say a little self-consciously.

Of course she uses bowls, like a civilized human in a house with people living in it.

"My mom and I…" I falter, then clear my throat and try again. "It's less cleanup if you go right for the carton."

Her eyes sparkle as she opens up the pint of Cherry Garcia. "I like that. Very pragmatic."

"But a little dangerous," I admit. "Before you know it, you hit the bottom of the pint."

"Totally worth it."

I can't help but agree.

She tosses the other flavors back in the freezer, then maneuvers onto the seat next to mine.

"Tell me about your schoolwork," Heidi prompts.

Although I don't get the impression that Heidi has some ulterior motive, I figured she didn't expect us to sit in silence.

This is a neutral enough topic that I engage her.

"I'm struggling through a history paper at the moment," I admit. "I breezed through my science work right away, but that and English have me struggling a bit."

"I would have thought with your crossword puzzle expertise that English was your favorite subject," Heidi says.

"Unfortunately, no. That kind of stuff…doesn't come easy for me."

"What kind of stuff?" Heidi asks.

I could open up to her, tell her all about how many times we moved and how schoolwork and assignments and essays overwhelm me, and just as I finally felt somewhat settled into a place, my mother died, and everything changed once again.

I shrug, and she senses the shift.

"Well, it seems like you've been settling in nicely," she says after a few beats, then she lets it all spill out. "I haven't wanted to bother you too much because I know you've been through a lot in such a short time, but Benjamin's horrible with the details; although, sometimes it's hard to believe given how much he can talk."

She stops herself to compose her thoughts.

"I want to see how you're doing, Avery."

I nibble a walnut piece off the spoon.

"I'm okay," I breathe.

"But it's okay...to not be okay, you know," Heidi says. "You don't have to hold everything in. No one expects you to put on a brave face. In fact, if anything, you're behaving the exact opposite of what we all expected."

And just like that, I'm no longer interested in the ice cream and bonding time—not that I was thrilled to participate in it to begin with.

I drop my spoon in the half-full carton and frown, thinking that Chunky Monkey isn't worth the tradeoff of whatever she's about to say next.

She clears her throat. "Anyway, I was thinking it might be a good time for us to clear the air."

"About how Benjamin and I were born within two days of each other, which means Trey likely hooked up with you and my mother within days of each other," I blurt out, hoping that my bluntness will make her shy away from the conversation.

Even then, I can't believe my own brazenness as the words fall out of my mouth. I expect her to be wildly offended or hurt, but she actually laughs.

"That's one way to put it," she says.

I wrinkle my nose at the thought, and somehow, I've managed to have a bigger impact on my own psyche than hers.

She looks a little sheepish before she says, "Carol suggested we wait until you approached us to talk about it, but I have a feeling that won't happen."

She's right about that.

"And maybe I should wait for Trey, seeing as I've already broached this and you're clearly uncomfortable—"

"No," I force out.

This is an awkward enough conversation with Heidi alone, and adding Trey into the mix would probably make it even worse.

"It's fine," I insist. "We can talk about it."

Heidi clears her throat. "Without getting into the details, Trey and I were young. And we had just gotten into a huge fight." She smiles sadly at the memory. "It coincided nicely with a boys weekend getaway to visit one of their friends in Pittsburgh, where they all got incredibly drunk and made not-so-great decisions."

"I think I can piece the rest together from there."

As much as I don't want to think about it, it's kind of impressive that my mother got pregnant with me, really, given the window of ovulation for a woman, the percentage chance of a condom failing, assuming they attempted to use protection, and...a few other factors I am too grossed out to consider.

"Trey came back to New York and immediately came clean about what happened," she explains. "And gave me the best apology I'd ever heard. It took some time, but we moved on and began planning our life together shortly after."

I drop my gaze to my hands. "And you didn't know about me? Neither of you did?"

"I knew about what happened that weekend, but no, nothing other than that," Heidi says, reaching over and holding my hand in hers.

Something about this maternal gesture—one I never thought I'd experience ever again—makes my chest want to crack open.

We're both a little sticky from the ice cream residue, but I couldn't care less, squeezing her fingers tighter and trying not to let the emotions break through my mental barriers.

"I don't know why your mother didn't reach out," Heidi continues, her voice a little lower than usual. "I can't imagine what she went through as a single mother, but I can see that she raised such a bright, beautiful young woman. I wish the circumstances were different, but I'm grateful you're in our lives."

At this, my throat grows thick, and as much as it hurts to swallow, I force myself to do so.

"You've been dealt an absolutely awful hand. Losing a parent is hard, I know. Both my parents died shortly after Trey and I got married. It wasn't unexpected like it was for you, but know that I can sympathize with what you're feeling and that we're here for you, for anything you need. You're going to work through your grief in your own way, but you don't have to do it alone."

All I can do is nod.

She sighs. "But I don't think that hiding up in your room is going to help heal anything, Avery."

"I'm not hiding," I admit.

"Then what are you doing?"

"I told you...I'm struggling. I'm behind in almost every class."

"So?" she says lightly.

I offer her what I hope is a look of skepticism.

"I've seen your SAT scores and transcripts, and they're strong enough that you're going to be more than fine, even if you take your foot off the gas a little. After all you've been through, you don't need to burn yourself out like this. It might give you a slight edge academically, but emotionally, I don't think it's worth the price you'll pay if you put yourself through it. Give yourself a break, Avery."

It reminds me of the last words my mother ever said to me. *"Maybe it's time we both started worrying a little less and living a little—"*

Even though they come from such different backgrounds, and we have drastically different relationships, I'm getting the same advice from both Heidi and my mother.

And maybe, just maybe, I should listen to it.

I can try it—not starting over, necessarily, but finding some middle ground between work and play. Like taking a break from pulling my hair out while trying to write a paper to have a little sugar and girl talk.

I pick up my spoon once more, a renewed appetite for Chunky Monkey and my life. "Less pressure, more ice cream."

"I'll cheers to that," Heidi says, holding up the end of her spoon.

I clink mine against hers, and we move to the terrace, spending the rest of the evening in a sugar coma and getting to know each other.

EIGHT

I feel like I've barely fallen asleep when I hear the creak of my bedroom door.

The silhouette of the person responsible for the noise is backlit against the hallway light, and the figure is far too tall to be Heidi and too thin to be Trey.

"Benjamin?" I roll over to turn on the light, confirming his presence.

"Avery," he says in a slightly slurred singsong voice. "Avery absent at absolutely A-plus...agh, evening."

He's wearing Caleb's non-prescription glasses, and as he staggers over, I notice there's some lipstick on the collar of his white button down.

The smell of alcohol and sweat on his skin makes me a little queasy, but he's unfazed by my reaction to his presence, as usual.

The grin from ear to ear tells me he's totally thrilled with how the night unfolded.

"Are you...drunk?" I ask incredulously.

I don't know if Trey and Heidi know of or approve of this behavior, but even then, I don't think they'll take kindly to being woken up at two in the morning by a very wired and swaying Benjamin, so I jump up and close the door behind him.

"No," he says. "Well, maybe. How many shots gets a person drunk?"

"I don't know," I admit.

I've never tried alcohol, and my mom never had a taste or room in our budget for it. Trey and Heidi have a glass or two of wine with dinner each night, commenting on the aromas and hints of flavors, not downing shots to loosen up like Benjamin does, apparently.

Benjamin finally makes it over to my bed and collapses on top of it, kicking off his shoes.

"Are you okay?" I ask through a yawn.

"I'm the best," he says.

I roll my eyes at that. "Clearly."

"Caleb, Ethan, and I went to this rooftop club downtown," he says too loudly for this time of night. "It was so crowded, like there were so many people and everyone was dancing and having the best time, and I think my favorite shot was the Lemon Drop...you can't even taste the alcohol."

I cross my arms on my chest. "I didn't take you for a lush, Benjamin. How did you even get into this club? And served alcohol?"

He reaches into his pocket and hands me his license.

"This says you're twenty-five." I eye my brother, who barely looks his actual age of seventeen.

"It's dark in all the places we go to," he explains like

he's a professional club hopper, "and if you slip a twenty with your ID, the bouncers don't look too closely."

"That kind of stuff only happens in movies," I say with a sigh.

"Because those movies are all based here."

I can't argue with that.

"I've already asked Caleb if his cousin in Toronto can get one for you made," Benjamin says excitedly. "You *have* to come out with us."

"Drinking isn't really my thing," I say.

"So? You don't have to drink if you don't want to. You can just come out and hang with us and dance."

He spreads out his arms like he's making a snow angel on my comforter. I don't even want to think about all the germs he has on his body that he is putting on my bed.

I try to imagine myself out with the boys, getting all dressed up and letting myself relax—worrying a little less and living a little.

It might be that my mother's words and Heidi's encouragement are both fresh in my mind, but I relent easily enough.

"Okay," I tell him.

"Yeah?" Benjamin perks up, expecting me to have declined outright.

"As long as we don't get in trouble with Heidi and Trey."

"And as long as you don't dance with guys."

"What?" I balk. "That's exactly what you just told me I'm supposed to do."

"I don't even know what I'm supposed to be doing,"

Benjamin says, "let alone being responsible for telling you what to do, little sis."

I shake my head and climb back under the covers, deciding that it's completely useless trying to reason with a drunk person.

Benjamin rolls over, leaving plenty of room for me, but makes no move to leave. "Caleb says I need to loosen up," he murmurs.

"Why?"

"Apparently I freak Brooke out whenever I try to talk to her."

I don't have to look at him to know he's running a hand through his messy hair, one of his signature moves.

"I just can't say or do anything right around her, and he thought going out tonight and being around other single females would help me."

I frown. "Did it?"

He laughs. "Not really. Or maybe it did. I don't know. We got mixed in with a group from NYU, and Ethan and I had a blast hanging out with them while Caleb supplied the alcohol and was in a texting fight with Sophia for most of the night."

"A texting fight?"

My question goes unanswered as he presses on with his preferred topic.

"Did you know we've gone to the same school since sixth grade, and I've never actually had a full conversation with Brooke Collins?" Benjamin says, still preoccupied with his own thoughts and concerns.

"No, I didn't know this."

"And then my sister swoops in and befriends her like

it's no big deal, not even putting in a good word for me when I've got your back."

"Hey! That's not exactly—"

"Most people suck anyway," Benjamin says with a sigh. "Especially the guys. You definitely don't want to talk to any of them. They're jerks. I already warned most of our grade that you're off-limits."

"You did what?" I demand.

"I did you a favor," he insists. "Well...I tried to. Bunch of assholes didn't even listen to me, so Caleb had to back me up."

I roll my eyes. "I can take care of myself, Benjamin. I don't need you to do anything for me, especially borderline sexist and weird protective stuff."

He stretches his arms upward. "I know I don't need to be, but I want to do it. Big brother stuff. You've been through enough and don't need to deal with these snob clown people. Just let me look out for you."

The gesture is nice, but speaking for me is not.

I've spent the last few days assuming people were skittish around me because of the ugly gash and whatever stories Sophia was spreading on my behalf.

"You told every single guy not to talk to me?"

"Yep," he says proudly. "Only Ethan and Caleb are the exceptions to that rule, but even then, I had to have a stern talking to them."

I can't even begin to imagine what "a stern talking to" qualifies as. "You don't trust your best friends?"

"You promised me you wouldn't date either of them," he reminds me.

"A promise I intend to keep."

He's contemplative for a few beats. "Ethan's trustworthy, but Caleb...no way. I've had the unfortunate privilege of listening to him talk about every single girl he's been even remotely interested in for our entire lives. He's a bit of an oversharer, and...you will not be one of those girls."

I roll my eyes. "So I suppose it goes both ways, then?"

"Hmm?"

"I'll tell every girl, including Brooke, you're off-limits."

He looks over at my smug expression and starts laughing. "Well played."

We fall into a rare silence, and I can hear his breathing level out.

"You know, having a sister isn't as bad as I thought it would be," Benjamin says, the sleepiness finally making his words slow and elongated.

I yawn and relax against the pillows. "You thought it would be bad?"

"That's a lie," he admits. "I didn't know what I thought. I didn't have enough time to really think it through because it all happened so fast."

"You're right about that," I say, already knowing he's close to sleep if he's not already out.

And it's true.

The death of a parent is enough to handle, let alone getting three new family members, a new city, and a new school thrown into the mix.

I've been reluctant to open myself up because I have nine months of living the life I never dreamed of...and then I'd be a legal adult and back into what I left behind. Surely the restaurant wouldn't hesitate to take me back, and I already debated on taking a round of general electives at a community college to help save money. It was all waiting for me back in Pennsylvania.

This life—this extraordinary privilege—was temporary.

After I turn off the light and start to fall asleep, I promise myself that I can't get used to it, that's for sure, but I think I can allow myself to live by my mother's, and Heidi's, advice. Or at least, I can try.

Hours later, when I wake up again, I'm on my own, and I breathe a sigh of relief.

I'm opening up to the idea of sibling bonding, but I'd prefer to do it during normal waking hours.

I rub the residual sleep out of my eyes and decide that if Benjamin's going to avoid personal boundaries by eating all my chocolate and storming in all hours of the night, I should probably start locking my door.

After I shower and dress, I head to the kitchen in hopes that Martha is in another waffle-making mood—she usually switches between waffles, bagels, pancakes, and toast. Even though Heidi and Trey don't like to eat carbohydrates in the morning, Benjamin usually eats what would be their portions and then some.

In the dining room, Trey is in his usual spot, fork in one hand, pen in the other.

We've established a routine—he ensures a hot cup of tea is waiting for me, then we tackle the puzzle while grazing on breakfast.

"Good morning," I say, grateful Martha made a waffle that takes up almost the entire plate I'm carrying in.

He smiles. "Good morning, Avery. Did you sleep well?"

Benjamin's snoring kept me awake for a little longer than I wanted, but I don't tell him that. "I did, thank you."

"Blood pressure as the heart contracts," Trey says, eyes on the paper. "Eight letters. First letter is S."

"Systolic," I say automatically.

He nods, then fills in the answer.

"You didn't know that one?" I ask, surprised.

"I just wanted to see if you did."

"Oh?"

"I understand that you and my wife had a discussion last night."

He's implying something very formal occurred, but we spent most of the time slurping down melted ice cream and gossiping about celebrities.

It was honestly not bad—kind of reminiscent of the nights my mother and I would spend together when we were somehow too exhausted to sleep. We'd watch reruns while she braided my hair, then we'd take turns painting each other's nails.

In the light of day, I decide I'm grateful that Heidi took the initiative to break the ice on that serious discussion. It was a conversation that needed to be had at some point, and now, we could move on.

But I did hope that sharing those words with Heidi meant I was spared from a repeat of it with Trey, but it appears I'm not that lucky.

"She mentioned that you're very interested in a medical profession," he adds.

I blink in surprise. It was a small footnote in our otherwise light conversation. I figured she'd fill him in on the details of our chat, but I'm surprised that's what he's leading with.

I regurgitate what I mentioned to her. "We took one of

those career tests during my freshman year. My love for science pointed me toward the medical field. I did my own research, and I think nursing might be a good fit, but I'm still figuring out the benefits of different programs or if community college is a better option."

He nods appreciatively. "Seems like you've given this some thought."

"A little bit," I say, not mentioning that I also spent most of my free time growing up binging every single streamable medical drama.

"Would you want to come to the office with me one of these days?"

"Like, to the hospital?" I clarify.

"Yes," he says with a hopeful smile. "It could help you decide what path you want to take. I could show you the administrative side of things, and you could shadow a few different departments and teams to see what you're interested in. Get real, on-the-job experience before you decide what you want to do for school."

It's a carrot, dangling in front of me, trying to smooth over our awkward relationship while pushing me forward to whatever's going to happen when I turn eighteen.

"I'd love to go." I don't have to feign enthusiasm for this response or when Heidi arrives to announce that the boys are going to take me out for a little adventure in the city today.

NINE

Riding the New York City subway is an event of itself.

I hold onto the little yellow card like it's gold, even after we've swiped through the turnstiles, finally depositing it in my purse once we've stepped through the train doors.

"Try not to touch the railings," Ethan advises, nodding his head to a guy who sneezes in his palm and then uses the same hand to hold onto the metal pole in the middle of the train car.

I spend the first ten minutes of the ride trying not to fall over.

Then I stare at the map that's enclosed in a frame right above a sleeping passenger, wishing I could trace all the little lines and colors that are like veins, running out from the heart of Manhattan.

I try to memorize all the stop names and get my bearings for the different parts of the city, but it's overwhelming.

Thankfully, we get to stay on the same train on the Q

line for the entire ride from the Upper East Side to Coney Island, which means we don't have to make a mad dash across a platform to catch another train like I see many other people do.

We wind our way toward lower Manhattan, then, eventually, cut across the East River over the Manhattan Bridge.

The boys roll their eyes and tease me when I pull out my phone to take pictures of the view.

I don't know how long you have to live here to lose an appreciation for this sort of stuff, but I can't imagine it will happen to me in the next nine months.

The hour-plus ride goes by quickly enough, with Benjamin's fidgeting increasing exponentially as we get closer.

Finally, we get to our stop, and as we leave the station, I'm hit with the overwhelming scent of grease and salty air. I breathe deeply, appreciating both.

Coney Island is famous even to someone like me, a girl from small towns around Pennsylvania who had no realistic plans of ever visiting the area.

The Fourth of July is always a slow day in the restaurant business, so I usually spend a few minutes of my shift watching the hot dog eating contest on television and wonder how many I can eat in ten minutes. It's not something I plan on trying anytime soon, even if we're at the right location for it.

It's a little cloudy today, and the wind picks up the closer we get to the water, sending a chill down my bare arms.

I can't believe we were just in the middle of concrete, and now we're here.

I guess people are supposed to come to the beach during the hottest months of the year, wearing their bathing suits and cool sunglasses, but I don't care that I'm not dressed for that.

I've never seen the ocean before—never dreamed of it, actually—and now, I can't take my eyes off it.

"So what do you want to do first?" Benjamin asks. "Bumper cars? Aquarium? Arcade? Rides? Hot dogs?"

"Beach," I say without hesitation.

He frowns and pushes Caleb's borrowed glasses up on the bridge of his nose. "It's not that great of a beach. I mean, you have to look out for broken glass every single step."

"I don't care. I want to see the ocean."

"It's not even really the ocean, technically. It's the Coney Island Channel."

"If you don't want to come with me, that's fine," I tell him, continuing my way forward.

"But—"

"I don't need you to babysit me, Benjamin. It's fine. Just text me where you're going, and I'll find you in a bit."

They've probably done this and the other more touristy things of the city dozens of times by now, but it's all new to me.

And I won't let the opportunity pass by.

"Avery, wait up," Ethan calls as he jogs toward me.

I slow my pace down to a leisurely stroll until he's by my side, aided by the gait of his long legs.

"Caleb and Ben are heading to Nathan's," he says, gesturing over his shoulder.

"You're not in the mood for a famous hot dog?"

He shakes his head. "Last time we were here, Ben ate five of them and then puked after one ride on the Cyclone."

"Gross."

Ethan looks at the entrance to Luna Park, the small amusement park in front of the beach, as we pass it, grimacing at the mental picture that is certainly surfacing in his mind.

"But I think this time, they need the fried food to help soak up the alcohol. They're both still a little hungover from last night."

"And you're not?" I ask curiously.

I imagine the three of them to split the amount of shots and trouble they get into equally, taking over whatever club they went to with the gusto awarded them by their fake IDs.

"Someone has to keep those two in line," Ethan says, shoving his hands in the pockets of his jeans while we walk.

It's ironic that when we first met, I considered him—with his long dark hair and closed-off stance—to be the edgy, rule-breaker type, when it appears he's the most responsible.

First impressions aren't everything, I guess, but I haven't forgotten the way both Caleb and Ethan's bright blue eyes locked on the gash down my face in shock.

To my relief, neither of them behave like I'm some charity case—even though that's pretty much what I am at this point—and seem just fine to have me tag along with them.

"You're coming with us next time, right?" His tone is

firm but curious, like he's trying to suss me out as a person just like I've been doing to him.

I nod, keeping my gaze fixed forward. "First beach, first ocean, first club," I say on an exhale.

"First experience of Ben's dance moves," Ethan adds.

"I don't know if I am mentally prepared for that one."

"It's a lot of jerky shoulder movements," he warns. "With the occasional erratic hip thrust."

"Erratic," I repeat, and instead of focusing on crossing the boardwalk, my mind is back to the stack of notecards I spent so much time with last summer.

"It means—"

"Having no fixed path."

He laughs. "We must have taken the same SAT prep course."

As if I'd be able to afford something like that. I did, however, find a list of recommended words online, along with a prep book that was only a few years old at our local library. The combination of the two helped boost my score by fifty points.

"Maybe," I say, not breaking my stride as I wrench off my flats, eager to stick my toes into the sand.

"You've really never been to a beach before?" Ethan asks, kicking off his shoes and socks.

"Nope. Never."

"I guess we're a little spoiled," he starts, and after my pointed look, adds, "Okay, a lot spoiled. But it's a good thing we're setting the bar low for you here. This is probably the worst beach experience you could ask for. Benjamin wasn't kidding about the broken glass."

From what I saw on television each year, I expected

hoards of crowds in costumes and screaming children, but there are only a handful of sunbathers and groups of families having picnics. In fact, Nathan's looked busier than this entire stretch of sand.

"It's less crowded than I thought it would be," I say as we slowly make our way to the water. "I guess it's late in the season."

He watches me take a few more steps forward until I'm right at the edge. "Take my word for it, Avery, your timing is perfect."

I sink into the wet, dark brown sand and stare at the horizon.

A handful of speed boats fly by, causing a ripple effect in the water, and I wait eagerly, watching wave after wave build up until, finally, the tide surges forward enough to touch my skin.

"Oh, it's cold," I yelp and jump backward, just out of reach.

Ethan laughs at my reaction.

After a few minutes of silence, I get brave enough to try it again, slowly making my way back into the standing water until it hits my ankles.

Ethan patiently waits for me to get bored with watching the waves, tentatively meeting them, and eventually splashing around.

"'I to the world am like a drop of water that in the ocean seeks another drop,'" Ethan says quietly, staring out at the horizon.

"What's that?" I ask.

He blinks, clearing his vision.

I don't think he intended to say those words loud enough for me to hear them.

"Shakespeare."

"You quote Shakespeare, while your brother runs around repeating lines from *Scrubs*?"

He laughs at that comparison. "To be fair, Caleb could probably recite *The Comedy of Errors* in its entirety if he wanted to. He has an eidetic memory and only needs to read something once before he has it down."

"Wow," I say. "I wish I had one of those."

"Sometimes I do, too, but I think it's overwhelming for him sometimes, which is why it's almost easier to ignore schoolwork and play mindless video games with Ben."

That makes sense, given on Thursday night Ethan and I stared at our homework while Caleb shrugged us off, saying schoolwork comes easy to him. It made me a little jealous, but I focused the energy into trying to salvage my own grades enough to have a solid future of my own.

"It'll come in handy when he ultimately goes to medical school."

"Definitely," he agrees. "Heidi calls us Right Brain and Left Brain sometimes because Caleb is driven by facts, numbers, and analyzing."

"And you're the creative one?"

"I want to be, but my parents love to remind me that there's not a lot of money in that."

I frown. "Does that mean it's not worthwhile? That pursuing something is only worth it if you can monetize it?"

He looks at me curiously, like no one has ever said something so obvious out loud to him before.

"Don't get me wrong, being poor really sucks," I continue, digging my toes in the sand. "As long as you can make a living and do what you want, who cares if you're a doctor or a painter or a server or a stay-at-home dad or anything else?"

I press my lips together, stopping the tangent.

"Sorry, you don't really need life advice from me, of all people."

"Don't apologize," he says, his expression contemplative as his eyes plead with mine.

This conversation is a little too deep considering there is a group of teenagers a few feet away listening to vulgar music.

"Come on," I encourage him. "Let's go find our hungover brothers."

"One second," Ethan says, bending down toward the sand.

I watch him carve his name into it, then I drop to do the same, marking my presence here, even though eventually someone else will step on it or the waves will wash it away.

"Well, now that I know you're going to be the next Shakespeare, I'm going to rely on you for even more help with our English assignments," I say lightly, shaking the excess sand from my palms as we walk back toward the boardwalk.

"I'll trade you for your help in anatomy," Ethan negotiates. "I've been lost since the first day of school."

"It's a deal."

We don't shake on it, but it still feels like we've affirmed a pact.

I have a feeling we will be spending a lot of time

together for the rest of the year doing homework while our brothers are messing around. I'm grateful to have a built-in resource for English, which is probably my most stressful subject.

Eventually, we track Caleb and Benjamin down in the arcade.

They're in the middle of an intense best-out-of-five game of air hockey, forcing Ethan and me to join them—siblings against siblings—and they all stand in shock when I send the puck through the goal within the first ten seconds.

"We should play pool next," I say simply. "Or darts."

I don't disclose that for the entire summer after I turned fourteen, my mom waitressed at a sports bar. I had to find some way to pass the time.

Ethan, most of all, does a terrible job at hiding the smile that forms on his lips. "Who are you?"

"My sister!" Benjamin exclaims, clearly excited to have someone coordinated on his side for once.

"Goal Five," Caleb offers.

Ethan swats his hand away. "Don't fraternize with the enemy."

"Let's make a bet!" Benjamin yells.

"What do you want?" Caleb asks.

Benjamin considers it. "How much cash do you have on you?"

"Benjamin," I say, surprised.

Caleb rifles through his wallet. "Thirty bucks."

"All of that toward William's Candy Shop," Benjamin says.

I don't know how Benjamin's teeth are so white and

intact with all the sugar he eats.

"And one study session a week on calculus for the rest of the semester," I add in boldly, desperate to tap into Caleb's brain.

"As the reigning middle school mathlete champion, you could work with no better person."

"Is that a real thing?" I ask.

"Have the trophy to prove it," Caleb says. "And if we win, you have to convince Sophia to swap with you to be my lab partner in anatomy."

"That's impossible," Benjamin sputters.

"It's fine," I cut in. "We're going to crush them."

Benjamin's confidence grows at my reassurance. "Hell yeah we are."

"Don't you want anything?" I ask Ethan.

He shrugs. "Listening to Caleb complain about Sophia even a fraction less is worth it."

Benjamin makes a show of cleaning the lenses of the glasses with the edge of his shirt, muttering about how it will help him focus on bringing his A-game. When he's satisfied, the four of us clink our paddles in the middle of the table and then we start what might be the most intense game I've ever played.

As I predicted, Benjamin and I—although, it's mostly just me—dominate every single game.

My brother is practically weighed down by the bag full of sweets that Caleb happily buys for everyone before heading to the beach.

We get sand and sugar all over ourselves as they give a play-by-play to one another of the games we just played. It's such a boy thing to do, but it's the first time I realize that I'm making lasting memories—not just for myself, because now, I'm a part of whatever they'll say when some random person asks when the last time they went to Coney Island was.

I'm becoming a character in their stories, and I don't know how I feel about it.

"I think," Benjamin says, officially giving up on chewing the caramel off his apple, "I'm ready to give the Cyclone another try."

Ethan eyes him warily. "I don't know. You just ate, like, three thousand calories of sugar. And as much as I enjoyed watching you puke the last time..."

"It's a hard pass for me," Caleb says.

Benjamin looks at me and pouts. "You'll go with me?"

"Okay," I give in easily.

He leads me, arm in arm, to the entrance of Luna Park, spouting facts about the history of the place—and his history with it.

As we stand in line, I tell him about the rides I rode at Cedar Point in celebration of my thirteenth birthday, and he is immediately jealous of all the record-setting coasters I've been on.

"Maybe we can do our joint birthday party there," he says, still clinging to the idea.

I press my lips together. "Maybe."

The Cyclone is, apparently, famous.

It was built almost one hundred years ago, and although it regularly gets work done, it feels like I'm zooming around to my death. I don't know if it's the fact that it's a wooden roller coaster or Benjamin's casual mention of the fatalities, but I don't relax during the entire ride.

Once it ends, I'm happy to see that Benjamin's normal pale coloring is in place, so I don't worry about having to practice my nursing abilities in the middle of the crowd. The people here are more eclectic than I'm accustomed to, and my eyes land on a surprising sight as we rejoin the twins.

"Hey, Caleb," I say. "Remember the *Scrubs* episode when they all go to the Bahamas for Janitor's wedding?"

"Of course." His tone comes off like he can't believe I would expect him to not remember such a pivotal storyline.

"'I got two words for you guys...banana and hammock,'" I quote, and he follows my gaze down toward the entrance of the park where an elderly man stands wearing a tiny bathing suit.

"Ugh," Caleb grimaces before he laughs. "I take back every Five I've given to you for that."

We wander through a few shops and stalls along the boardwalk before we eventually give up on exploring because we're all exhausted and ready to head home.

I feel more confident as we board the train this time, and since we're at the end of the line, all four of us can snag seats.

Despite Ethan's warning on the way here not to touch anything, he sits down beside me, and we spend the first few stops watching Caleb and Benjamin argue over who looks better in Caleb's glasses.

"For the record, I think it's Ben," Ethan whispers to me.

And for the first time since I woke up in the hospital, I feel like I want to smile.

TEN

In an effort to not monopolize the boys' time—and frankly, to get a break from their antics—I try to spend more time with Brooke.

The awkwardness I felt at pursuing a friendship dissolves almost as soon as it surfaces. And it's mostly because she seems just as eager to talk to me, someone who isn't the typical Manhattan rich kid norm, matching her down-to-earth vibe.

I'm also happy that she seems perfectly content to sit in silence beside me and do homework during our lunch hour, which means I'm free almost every evening to watch the boys play video games or work on my rewatch of *Grey's Anatomy*. I've been obsessing over it ever since Heidi added the Netflix account to the television in my room.

In the first few weeks of being in New York, I begin to find contentment in the state of affairs, only to be thrown for a loop after Brooke and I finish up a worksheet on the endocrine system.

"Do you have plans on Saturday night?" Brooke asks me, twirling her pen nervously in her hand.

I think she knows by now that I never have plans, but it's nice that she is polite enough to ask.

"No," I say. "Why?"

"I was thinking we could have a girls night at my house. Chick flicks, nail painting, man hating, that kind of thing."

It doesn't sound so awful.

Plus, I'm sure that all the Carters and the two Navarro boys could use a break from checking in on me and obsessing over my well-being.

"What can I bring?" I ask.

"You live by Sprinkles, don't you?" Sophia asks, joining our table.

I didn't realize she was invited, but I shouldn't be surprised. Brooke has more female friends than just me, of course, so it makes sense that she'd be included.

"I think so," I say, trying to decide if that name sounds familiar.

"A dozen assorted cupcakes, please," Sophia says with an innocent smile.

"Does she look like a delivery service to you, Soph?" Brooke asks with a glare before she turns to me. "You don't have to bring anything other than yourself."

Even with her encouragement, I don't want to show up empty-handed, so when seven o'clock on Saturday rolls around, I knock on the door of her apartment while juggling a box of cupcakes and a bottle of sparkling rose seltzer that Heidi enthusiastically pawned off on me.

She was thrilled to hear that I had plans with friends and drilled me with questions that I tried my best to answer patiently, recalling her comment about how Benjamin doesn't really indulge her with any interesting details.

An older version of Brooke opens the door and ushers me inside.

"You must be Avery," she says, her eyes laser focused on the healing scar. "I've heard so much about you these past few weeks."

I've never known what to say when someone uses that line because in most cases, it's said by someone I've heard little to nothing about.

"Thank you," I return.

"The girls are down the hall. Have fun!"

I kick off my shoes and manage to not drop anything when I push open her door.

"Avery's here!" Brooke announces, jumping up to help me.

Her room is a complete explosion of pink—carpet, walls, bedspread, furniture—and it takes a second for my eyes to adjust.

Sophia swiftly takes the box of cupcakes out of my hands and helps herself to one of the red velvets.

"So good," she says, mouth already staining red.

Brooke laughs at how ridiculous she looks, teasing her lightly about being an animal while Sophia wipes her lips with the back of her hand.

I take a seat on the floor in their little circle, not totally relaxing as they keep up their banter.

I'm a little nervous about this entire endeavor. I'm still barely comfortable in my bedroom at the Carters' house, and it just seems like we're intentionally crossing a line of schoolmates to...friends. But these people around me seem to want that—connecting on a deeper, more personal level.

Part of me still thinks I should continue to push my emotions down instead of opening up and finding attachment to any person or place, letting myself be vulnerable, even though I don't think I'm strong enough to bear another loss at this point.

After the talk with Heidi, I stopped doing everything I could to block everything and everyone out.

Every single day, I try to lower my barrier just a little bit more, and this night might be what causes it to drop completely.

That thought scares the hell out of me.

"I brought Taco Bell!" an excited voice screeches behind me.

Emily, who I recognize from my English class, bursts into the bedroom.

As the girls are caught up in a whirlwind of excited giggles in anticipation of the carbohydrates, I feel my phone buzz for the fifth time since I sat down.

I check my phone, concerned that something is genuinely wrong, only to roll my eyes at the screen.

Benjamin keeps texting me, begging for regular updates and vivid descriptions of every single thing we talk about that can some way relate to him.

I stick my phone back in my bag, deciding to pretend for the time being that I haven't seen his messages.

"You're a dumbass for only getting one chicken quesadilla," Sophia argues with Emily.

"Let's just split it, then," Emily suggests as Brooke tosses me a soft taco.

"This is such a treat," Brooke gushes in excitement.

The school dining hall serves better food than most restaurants I've been to, but somehow, this meal is an indulgence. Still, I don't complain about it as I unwrap it and take the first bite.

Sophia balks at Brooke, who is rapidly tearing open the wrapper on her food. "I thought you weren't eating meat after the frog dissection."

"It's a bean burrito," she retorts proudly.

"Gross," Sophia says.

"Well whatever you think it is, you better appreciate it," Emily says. "I had to go all the way to Midtown to get it."

Sophia rolls her eyes. "You live in Soho. It's on the way up here, anyway."

"Then on Monday, you won't mind bringing me coffee from that little shop we went to in Kips Bay?" Emily poses, earning a huff from Sophia.

I don't think I'm going to live here long enough to understand this argument.

"I think you guys are speaking Greek to Avery," Brooke says, catching how lost I am at the mention of all these places I haven't been. "New subject."

"It's fine," I insist.

I don't want to cause anyone's unhappiness. If they want to argue about this for the next four hours, who am I to stop them?

"I keep forgetting you're new here," Emily says.

I don't doubt her sincerity, but I don't think that's actually true.

People at school seem to be growing more accustomed to me, judging solely by the fact that I'm getting far fewer stares—but I'm still getting enough where I'm reminded of the scar on my face.

My not belonging in this world is at the forefront of my mind every single day.

"So you really had no idea that you had this brother and father and stepmom until the accident?" Sophia pries, diving right into a personal question, even though we barely know each other, before she chomps down on a loaded nacho chip.

Brooke's eyes go wide, ready to defend me if needed, but I sigh—given how good Sophia has been for the rumor mill at school, I might as well confirm the truth.

"No idea," I admit. "I blacked out at the accident and woke up to this whole new life. New place. New family. New school."

And I didn't have a choice in any of it.

"Wow," Emily breathes.

"It's kind of like one of those movies where the girl finds out she's secretly a princess," Sophia says. "The Carters are practically New York royalty."

Despite their gobs of money and lavish apartment, they seem very normal to me.

"Yeah, because you're out here slumming it," Brooke teases.

Sophia tries to hold a pout but ultimately joins in Brooke and Emily's giggles at her expense.

"In all fairness, my father would never buy me that," she says, pointing to the purse Heidi picked out for me.

I trace the little buckle on the front of it, wondering if she committed some stepmother faux pas with her choice. Maybe it's out of season or something...I don't know, and I don't really care. It holds my stuff, and that's good enough for me.

"Why's that?" Emily asks.

Sophia's eyebrow lifts, surprised that her friend doesn't know the answer to that question.

"Because it's Hermes." After seeing my non-reaction, she adds, "And it's, like, ten thousand dollars."

I tear my hands away from it, as if I shouldn't be allowed to touch something that cost more than a year's worth of rent in our Pittsburgh apartment.

"I see why Ethan likes you," Sophia admits, popping the lid on one of the ramekins of cheese sauce.

"What?" I balk at her casual insinuation. "What do you mean?"

"Oh, come on, you two are always hanging out, using big words, doing homework, and whatnot."

I don't think I give him more attention than I give anyone else, but we have kept the promise we made to each other to help with schoolwork, which means we spend a lot of time together.

"It's not like that," I insist. "And besides the fact that we're just friends, Benjamin told all the guys in school not to talk to me and made me swear to him that I'd never date any of his friends."

"Why did he do that?" Brooke asks.

I shrug. "I don't know, but he was pretty adamant about it."

Emily's smile falters, and Sophia bursts out laughing.

"What?" I ask, not understanding the reaction from either of them.

"In eighth grade, Emily had the biggest crush on Caleb," Sophia starts. "Remember, Brooke?"

Emily pouts. "Oh, come on, you're going to make Avery hate me before she even knows me."

"No, no, no," Sophia says. "This is a story that needs to be told for context and mocking. So, Emily had this big crush on Caleb, right? And decided the best way to do it would be to become friends with Ben and Ethan, trying to get 'in' with them to get close to Caleb. Well, it turned out that all three of them liked Emily, but Caleb asked Marcia Bennett to the eighth grade dance because he didn't want to get in between anything."

"And then it all blew up in the middle of the dance," Brooke finishes for her. "A spectacular fight between the three of them, and Emily cried in the bathroom for the rest of the night."

"So, at what point did you and Caleb get together?" I ask Sophia.

"Sophomore year," Sophia says sourly. "But I wish it was never."

"Those sound like song lyrics," I tell her.

"Well, 'Avery and Ethan' does kind of sound like a band name," Brooke says. "Much better than 'Sophia and Caleb,' at least."

Emily snorts. "The only band with more contentious breakups than Sophia and Caleb is probably, like, The Smiths or Oasis or something."

Brooke turns to me. "They've been getting back together and breaking up for two years."

"That's not true," Sophia says.

"It most definitely is," Brooke insists.

"Well, whatever, this time it's definitely sticking." The confidence with which she says it makes me believe her wholeheartedly, but the skepticism on Brooke and Emily's faces poses doubt. "I will not have my senior year ruined by all our constant fighting. It's just exhausting."

Emily laughs. "For you and me both."

Sophia ignores her jab and turns her tone to be more serious and resolute. "Look, I think we both have finally realized that we keep repeating the cycle because we care about each other but just aren't right for each other. And then we both get lonely and fall right back into it, and that's not really fair to either of us."

"That's actually...very mature," Brooke admits.

"I'm going to try to not be offended at your tone. So, anyway, I've joined a few dating apps and—"

"You have to let me swipe for you." Emily grabs Sophia's phone, and before I understand what is happening, they both busy themselves with making commentary on each guy's profile.

"Do you miss your old friends?" Brooke asks me, ignoring the other two.

It feels like every single time someone asks me a question, my answer is something kind of depressing, which makes me frown.

It's not that my life with my mother was unhappy—in fact, we had a lot of fun together—but it wasn't as glamorous and eventful as the lives of my schoolmates now. And now, I can barely talk about her without threatening to tear myself open.

"We moved around a lot," I say, trying to explain my lack of friends in the easiest way.

It wasn't that I was totally without social interaction. There was always plenty of drama at the restaurant, and occasionally I'd make a friend at school if I stayed long enough to get invested, but things always dwindled off when we eventually moved again.

These girls, and the boys at home, all grew up together. They have years upon years of memories and friendship to comfort them. And I'm being shoved into it.

It feels like trying to put toothpaste back in the tube after you've accidentally pressed out too much onto your toothbrush.

"Well, I'm glad you're here," Brooke says with a smile.

"Yeah, I need another opinion on this," Sophia says to Emily, shoving her phone in front of my face. "What do you think?"

I still can't decide if she hates me or not—and I feel myself starting to care about that answer.

ELEVEN

Carol from Social Services calls the next day, and I answer while I sit on the counter in my bathroom and stare at my scar.

She apologizes for interrupting my weekend, saying she's just eager to check in on how I'm doing.

I have a feeling Heidi tipped her off about my newfound social life.

As if her randomly interrupting my new attempt at normalcy isn't enough of a reminder of what I've gone through, she wants details. About school. About friends. About the dynamic with Heidi and Trey. About how I'm living and sleeping and coping.

After twenty minutes of mostly one-word answers on my part, she reminds me she's here to help, and that I shouldn't hesitate to reach out if I need anything or want to open up to anyone.

I thank her but hang up the phone as soon as I can.

Heidi and Trey have been nice, but their method of

ensuring I'm okay means hovering constantly, either themselves or putting someone else up to the job.

And after a night with Sophia, Brooke, and Emily, and another intrusion by Benjamin demanding every single detail of our conversation, I'm feeling a little drained.

It should be a pleasant feeling, having these people invested in me, but I need a break.

The pressure is growing, and I want to escape momentarily to be just another nameless face in the crowd, not some damaged girl whose mother died.

I scribble a note that I'm going for a walk, then slide it under Heidi and Trey's bedroom door. It might be easier to just knock and ask for permission to go out, but I don't want to set that precedent. And I definitely don't want to give anyone else a chance to join me in getting some air.

Excitement bubbles in my chest as I step out of the elevator.

I keep my head down, wanting to avoid a conversation with Rick, but I gasp when I see him and Martha together, locked in an embrace behind his desk—I guess the boys were right about this speculation, and I can't help but smirk.

I slip out, unnoticed, through the propped-open front door.

The moment my lungs take in the fresh fall air, I know that wandering the streets of New York is the therapy I need right now.

I walk along the city sidewalks, appreciating the dull roar of traffic and people talking. I look at each advertisement on the top of the yellow cabs while I wait for the walk signal to turn—although there are more experienced people around me who cross before it's our turn, but I'm not that brave.

Being a rule follower to a fault should have protected me from bad things.

We always paid our rent on time.

Showed up at our shifts when we were supposed to.

Claimed exactly the amount of tips we made.

And followed the traffic signals.

Unfortunately, not everyone plays by the same rules, and it's because one person drunkenly ran a red light that I no longer have a mother.

I cross through Central Park, slowly taking in the fall weather and background noise of people chatting, listening to music, and enjoying the afternoon. The trees are mostly a yellow hue, and every so often the wind picks up, sending a few errant leaves floating down toward the ground.

The path leads me toward a playground that looks like a cement fort surrounded by a metal fence, almost as if it's a castle protecting the children inside.

My feet stop at the entrance, and I can't help but watch the children running around playing tag, laughing and screaming.

I think about a little park my mom used to take me to when I was a kid. It was just a set of swings, a slide, and monkey bars—it seems pathetic compared to this one, which was probably designed by an actual architect.

My eyes are drawn over toward the parents, who seem happy to socialize with other adults while their kids are preoccupied.

I can't recall if my mother got the same reprieve from

me as a child, and as far as I remember, she never went on any dates or had any friends outside of work.

Our lives were so focused on surviving that we didn't really get a chance to live. She was optimistic that, eventually, we'd break through it, but she didn't get to see it.

I tear my eyes away from the scene and start walking again, trying to ignore the burn in my throat.

When the hot tears overflow and trickle down my face, I wipe them away angrily, taking a deep breath to clear my mind of everything but the commitment to putting one foot in front of the other.

And for as anonymous as I wanted to be in the crowd, too often I see gazes linger on my cheek. Each casual glance is like a tug at an open wound.

Eventually, it's all too much, and I collapse onto a bench and pinch my eyes closed, willing the moment of weakness to pass.

This is probably why Heidi, Trey, and everyone else tries to keep my mind preoccupied, staying so busy that I can't focus on what is missing.

But to remember the happy memories with my mother, I have to learn to cope with the pain.

"Avery?"

I open my eyes and blink to clear my vision.

Ethan pulls his headphones from his ears. "Are you okay?"

I take a deep breath. "I don't know."

He sits down beside me, eyes raking over my face.

I'm sure my eyes are puffy and my cheeks are splotchy, but I don't care—my appearance doesn't matter to me until

I catch him staring at my scar, which is like a punch to the gut.

I quickly pull my hair down and turn, forcing his gaze away.

I know I can't blame him or anyone else for eyeing my Frankenstein gash. Humans are drawn to the abnormalities in life, and his good looks stand out to me just as much as my scar does to him—but I've let him into my life enough that somehow it feels like a betrayal when he sees me just like everyone else does.

To his credit, he says nothing, but I can feel his gaze on my unmarred side as I stare at the ground.

"Cat scratches," he says simply.

He shrugs his arm out of his jacket, pulling my attention to his forearm and the three thin scars that run diagonally across the back of his wrist.

"I always wanted a dog," he continues. "But somehow Caleb talked my mom into getting a cat. I think the damn thing knew it, too. It never liked me. I can't say I was too disappointed when it ran away last year, but don't tell Caleb or Ben."

He flips his arm, showing me the center of his palm with a few small dots healed in the center.

"Pickup football game in the park a few Thanksgivings ago. I didn't expect the person I was guarding to be wearing spikes." He smirks. "Or to be so angry at losing that he would step on my hand in retaliation."

He turns away slightly and lifts the edge of his shirt to show a thin line on his back, which doesn't look all that different than my appendectomy scar.

"Your brother stabbed me with a steak knife. We were

seven and playing ninjas." He releases the fabric from his fingertips, but my eyes still linger on the spot. "I still won," he adds smugly.

Whatever emotion I'm failing to hide on my face causes his eyes to flash.

His jaw clenches with resolve before he turns back to face me and slowly lifts the front of his shirt until the hem hits his neck.

My eyes move more slowly than they should as he bares himself to me, but he's patient, waiting until my gaze lands on the thick healed scar that's cut down the entirety of his sternum.

I know enough to understand that he's had major surgery.

"I've got troubles of the heart," he says, romanticizing the notion that his chest was once split open. "Specifically of the aortic valve."

Someday my scar's going to be like his, light pink and blended, but for now, it's still a little red, healing, and angry.

Instinctively, I reach out to run my fingertips along the line of his chest, but I stop myself when I realize what I'm doing.

I glance up at him, an apology on my lips, but he swallows, and instead of speaking, I watch the movement of his throat.

Finally, he releases his shirt. "So, yeah, we all have scars," he says. "'He jests at scars that never felt a wound.'"

I find my voice enough to ask, "More Shakespeare?"

He nods, pressing on like he hasn't just bared himself to

me. "There's a quote for everything, and I've memorized far too many of them."

"Is that how you spend your Sunday afternoons?" I ask coyly, noting that my throat is still just a little thick.

"Sometimes," he admits. "But it's just nice to be outside."

I glance around in appreciation and take a deep breath, forcing my body to relax on the long exhale. "It's beautiful here."

"You think this is nice?" Ethan challenges. "Come on, I'll take you to my favorite spot."

He stands and offers his hand.

I stare at the gesture like it's some alien offering, but my body complies eventually, sliding my fingers through his.

I'm still trying to get my bearings in the city, but I think he's leading us farther south, or maybe in toward the middle of the park.

As we walk, I try not to dwell on how warm and rough his skin is, or how our interlaced fingers fit together perfectly.

"How was girls night?" Ethan asks in an amused tone, breaking the silence between us.

"It was...interesting. Lots of gossiping, snacking, and plotting for world domination."

"Much better than boys night, which was just mostly playing video games and listening to Ben's whining and speculating about your night while Caleb and Sophia continued their ongoing text-fight."

Sophia insists that they're definitely broken up, but it

seemed like every five minutes his name popped up on her phone screen.

"I think next weekend will be better," Ethan says.

"Why's that?"

"Benjamin didn't tell you? We're taking you to the club for Halloween. My cousin, Chris, came through with your fake ID in record speed."

"Oh." Given that I'm still a little emotional, I know that alcohol isn't the best thing to add into the mix, so I'm not totally enthused by the idea at this exact moment.

"I thought you wanted to go?"

"Are your parents okay with you going out?" I deflect.

"Caleb and I are eighteen."

"And yet I'm sure your identification puts you somewhere in your twenties."

He laughs. "You're not wrong. But they really don't care what we do as long as we don't get in any trouble. Trey and Heidi are the same way. Besides, I'm pretty sure they're all going to some event or dinner or something on their own, so they won't even notice."

I'm not totally sold on the idea, but I don't vocalize it because Ethan stops moving and drops my hand.

I feel the loss more than I should.

"Here," he says, gesturing around us.

We're standing on top of a hill that's not tall—especially given that I grew up driving around the mountains of Western Pennsylvania—but it's at a perfect point in the middle of Central Park that the views are incredible.

I turn in place, marveling at how the trees abruptly end and the massive buildings shoot up into the sky. It's a stark contrast, and I'm awed by the beauty.

Just like when we were at the beach, he watches me as I revel in my surroundings, like he's enjoying my reaction just as much as I'm enjoying the new experience.

"You should see it at night," Ethan says. "Although there are pretty good views from your terrace."

"And not from yours?"

"You have an unobstructed view, and even though we have the same layout of our apartment, our terrace is a lot smaller. My room is right below yours, and Caleb and Benjamin's are stacked on top of each other."

Even though he said it casually, it felt like kind of an intimate admission.

"Really?" I ask.

"When we were kids, we wanted to drill a hole from Benjamin's room to Caleb's and put in a fire pole, but our parents said no."

"That probably would make it easier to sneak out and go to clubs."

His eyes flash. "So does that mean you're coming?"

"I guess," I say, a ringing endorsement.

Regardless of my tone, he smiles, then fills me in on what a typical night out is like, distracting me as we walk back by the playground and wind our way home.

TWELVE

The club is within walking distance from our building, and it's weird that within a few blocks from our pristine apartment is a dark, crowded, hot club.

When I say that out loud, the boys just shrug it off, not really amused by the contrast of it like I am, and I think it's because they're all eager to get inside and on with the night.

The bored bouncer at the door barely glances at my identification, but his eyes rake over the amount of leg that I'm showing in this little black strappy dress. It's far more than I usually do, but it was the only dress in my newly filled closet that seemed appropriate.

Heidi was thrilled to hear that we were all going out for Halloween—although I don't think Benjamin gave her the exact details of our plans—and wanted to help me with my costume.

Or rather, she talked me into wearing this dress and doing very heavy eye makeup, insisting that it's more about having fun and breaking out of the norm than being dressed in a costume.

To complete the ensemble, she dug a witch's hat out of storage, which currently sits on Benjamin's head. It doesn't really make sense since he's supposed to be James Bond, but at least the black hat matches his tuxedo.

Caleb is completely decked out in a pirate costume; although, the bouncer confiscated his pirate sword at the door.

Ethan insists he is dressed as a biker. I'm pretty sure he's wearing the same jeans and boots he always does, but instead of a hoodie, he's wearing a leather jacket that has many girls eyeing him and his long hair.

"Drinks?" Benjamin yells excitedly, bouncing to the beat of the music.

The lights flash overhead as the crowd in front of the booth screams for whatever song the DJ just put on, and I turn my back, wondering if it's possible to seriously damage my eardrums by visiting one dance club.

"Cool, isn't it?" Caleb says, looking around at all the people lowering their inhibitions.

The space is much better than I expected, with multiple bars and dance floors, and I try my best to take it all in at once.

Most people are paired off, dancing and moving to the beat of the music, but there's a ring of people around the bar who are socializing and tossing back shots—I'm going to have to do a lot of the latter to get the courage to be a part of the former.

"What do you want to drink?" Benjamin asks, expecting the bartender's approach.

"Whatever," I say.

"Better get a few rounds," Caleb says. "It's getting crowded."

A few girls are checking out Caleb and Ethan—and me, the presumed competition—while the bartender pours several fresh drinks for us, lining them up on the bar.

I stick close to Benjamin as the girls try to pull the twins into conversation, but they're solely focused on the shots he's trying to hand over without spilling.

"This is a Lemon Drop," Benjamin yells at me. "It's vodka. That's okay?"

"Sure," I say with a shrug, hoping that it actually will be.

The four of us cheers and then toss them back.

The boys do it with far more expertise than me, and although the lemon taste cuts the alcohol, I still have to suppress the urge to cough.

None of us hide our winces, though.

"It gets better after the first one," Benjamin promises as his eyes water.

And I absolutely don't believe him.

In between the boys talking and laughing, we each throw back another shot.

I'm already just out of control enough that I decline the third one when it's offered.

Benjamin happily shoots it back on my behalf, then he turns his attention to the dance floor, dragging me along with him.

He's all up in my personal space, and for once, I appreciate it. This crowd is like quicksand, sucking us in and forcing us to move to stay afloat.

I move my hips to the pounding bass while Benjamin attempts to put swing dance moves on me.

We keep bumping into couples who are dancing more closely and vulgarly than I've ever seen before. I couldn't mimic them if I tried—my body wasn't made to twerk or do whatever that is.

But I think I'm having fun.

It's hard not to, given that my muscles have lost their rigidness, courtesy of the alcohol and Benjamin's dance moves.

As I'm swung around for the twentieth time, I see that the twins are busy, each indulging a girl in her request to dance.

"Don't you want to dance with someone else?" I ask Benjamin.

He purses his lips and shakes his shoulders to emphasize the finger guns he's pointing upward. Whether that's a dance move or a James Bond tribute, I'm not exactly sure. But he's too lost to the beat of the music, yelling along to a song I don't recognize, which is fine by me—I need a break from being jerked around by him.

I'm about to make an excuse to go off and find the bathroom when Ethan reaches out, sidestepping his dance partner to pull me toward him.

"Please?" he says in my ear. "This girl won't leave me alone."

I go rigid, knowing this is absolutely not a good idea.

Since our little walk and scar sharing in Central Park, I've felt connected to him in a deeper way than everyone else in my life here.

All week, we've been locking eyes—in English class, at

lunch, while doing our homework, and just hanging out after school.

It seemed innocent enough at first, but now, I'm starting to look for him everywhere I am.

Looking is harmless in theory, but catching each other's gazes is problematic—and touching each other just seems flat-out dangerous.

Ethan doesn't wait for my answer, though.

He slides his hands around my waist and turns me outward so I'm pulled flush against him.

I glance at Benjamin for help, but he has two girls who are completely enthralled by his attention and dance moves, and I also note that Caleb is dancing a little dirty with his latest partner, who is nearly bent over.

The music, in combination with the alcohol, lights, and costumes, is to blame for our lowered inhibitions.

That's *definitely* it, I tell myself.

Ethan moves us slowly to the rhythm, and I melt into him.

I'm thankful that those two shots have loosened me up to the point where being self-conscious has dropped a few notches on my list of thoughts at the moment.

Through the guise of music, I relax even more, letting my back fall onto his chest completely.

His hands roam freely up and down my sides, sliding along all the lines and curves of my body.

I've never been touched like this, and it feels almost too good, like I'm not capable of containing the heat and wanting that grow inside me.

In a moment of bravery, I reach up behind me with one hand, steadying myself on him as I move my hips.

I decide that I love dancing.

Everything blurs around us as we keep up this pace and movement through a few songs.

Through the pulse of the music, Ethan and I are shuffled away from Benjamin and Caleb. It's not intentional, and I don't even notice it at first. When I do, I know I should stand my ground, crane my neck, and look for them, but I'm pulled in deeper—to the crowd, to the rhythm, to him.

Everyone around us throws their hands up in the air, screaming the lyrics and letting themselves go.

They're succumbing to the music the way I wanted to give myself over to the city last weekend. I tried to find a momentary reprieve from everything and just exist, but instead, I found Ethan, who has been hiding in plain sight all along.

Ethan spins me around to face him.

Our eyes meet as we continue moving together, and holy hell, it's intimate.

I can see it all now—the intensity of how he feels at this moment, how selfish he's being in having free rein over me, and how he's holding on in hope that I won't let go.

In an overwhelming moment of emotion, my brain goes on the fritz, diving into a powerful memory I've run through too many times recently but hadn't planned on focusing on tonight.

My cheeks grow red and hot as I sense her knowing smile. "I'm too busy for a relationship."

"Who says you need to have a relationship with him?"

"Mom!" I laugh. "Shouldn't you be advocating for me to stay on track with school, work, and college applications?"

The light turns green, and she chuckles as she speeds up through the intersection. "Maybe it's time we both started worrying a little less and living a little—"

It was the last conversation my mother and I had before my life crashed and burned, and it's the one I keep coming back to, as if her last wish was for me to be a little reckless.

And I guess it shouldn't feel out of place.

If anything, it's good timing for that memory to resurface, given that not one single part of my body agrees with the rational, self-preserving part of my brain.

I renew my grip on Ethan's shoulders and take in how brutally gorgeous he is. His blue eyes, cut jawline, and long hair is a killer combination, but my attraction is deepened by the way he seems to see me in a way no one else does.

I have a decision to make.

Am I going to stay in this emotionless void, holding everything in until I'm back in my old life in Pennsylvania in June? Or am I going to allow myself to actually feel something and deal with the consequences later?

"Consequences," I say out loud.

Ethan can't hear me over the music, so he bends down slightly, silently asking me to repeat myself in his ear.

My hand moves to his chin, holding him in place as I stand on my tiptoes and kiss him.

I always hoped my first kiss would be in some romantic fashion, like at the top of a Ferris wheel or with some long-term boyfriend I always planned to find someday, but it's in the dark corner of a club when I'm a little tipsy.

Ethan is stunned at first, then he drives all the momentum forward, pulling me into him completely.

He parts my lips quickly with his tongue, owning the

pressure and movement between us, and I'm more than happy to give up the control at the moment.

His lips are soft and warm, moving deliberately over mine.

I feel the urgency and the relief in his kiss, almost like he never expected it to happen but isn't planning on letting it go to waste now that it is happening.

I gasp as he winds his hands in my hair, holding me steady as his kiss trails from my mouth to my neck, then catch the glimpse of a smile before his lips are once again on mine.

But I don't just feel him on my mouth—this urgency shoots through my body all the way down to my toes, and I soon become addicted to the closeness and the friction between us.

He nips at my bottom lip, and I'm grateful that the music drowns out the sound of the moan in my throat.

It's too much, like it's the most alive I've ever been—every muscle, tendon, and part of my body is humming with a need for more.

In just these few moments of kissing Ethan, I'm addicted, and I can't help but wonder why I haven't done this sort of thing sooner.

Because I never had the chance until now.

And I probably wouldn't have if the worst hadn't happened.

That thought jars me back to reality, and I break the kiss.

My cheeks flush with embarrassment at how I was practically clawing at him in a crowd of people, even though everyone around us appears lost in their own little lust-fueled movements.

I breathe, trying to pull myself out of this spiral, but it doesn't work until my eyes lock with Ethan's bright blue ones.

He's clearly stunned—by my making the move in the first place or pulling away from him so abruptly, I'm not sure—but his hold on my hips is resolute.

And he looks like he wants to do it all over again.

I thought kissing him would be as simple as indulging an impulse, and that once I gave in, I would be done. It was supposed to be the result of just getting caught up in the moment, but it feels like my entire body has been exposed to a live wire.

I can't help but wonder if he felt it, too.

Without asking permission, I reach back up and pull down the neck of his plain white shirt.

Ignoring his confused look, I don't stop gripping the fabric until I can see the top of his scar.

I place a light kiss on it, then step back, pressing my entire hand against the length, feeling his heart beat rapidly under my palm.

Ethan's chest hitches as I slide my thumb up, running it along his collarbone.

If we weren't in such a public setting, I think I would demand to see more of him, but instead, I drop my hand from his chest and bring it to my lips, surprised to feel that they're a little swollen.

"There they are," Caleb's voice calls over the music.

Ethan runs a hand through his hair but doesn't let his

gaze drop from mine, trying to have some sort of unspoken conversation with me that I don't even try to comprehend.

I turn away on shaky legs and see that, thankfully, Caleb and Benjamin don't look surprised or suspicious when they finally get to us.

It's clear they have absolutely no idea what just occurred between us, and if I am being honest with myself, I don't exactly know what happened either.

But I want to do it again.

THIRTEEN

Kissing Ethan was definitely a mistake.

I wasn't sure what to expect as I waited for him to show up for breakfast the next morning—like he always does on the weekends—but it wasn't for him to barely acknowledge my existence.

By all other accounts, it's a normal breakfast.

We all sit in our usual spots, ignoring both Heidi and Trey's comments about how we're suspiciously quiet this morning. They're also pretending like Martha didn't leave us all two ibuprofen tablets next to our large glasses of water.

But I feel a change.

I guess it's a good thing I've had a lot of practice suppressing my emotions, but I keep everything inward easily enough, pretending that those minutes in each other's arms last night wasn't gut-wrenchingly vulnerable.

To distract myself, I indulge Heidi's questions about what homework I'm working on today, and she tells us all about how she and Trey were judges for the costume contest at whatever party they went to last night.

It doesn't really work, though, because as she chatters happily, I stare at Ethan.

We've moved past dangerous territory and right into dire—another vocabulary word—circumstances.

This realization is an odd feeling, though, like I'm standing at the edge of the cliff, trying to decide if I want to jump.

And I think Ethan knows that I might not be ready to fall just yet, even if he's acting as a parachute.

When Benjamin reaches over to swipe my bacon like usual, I'm reminded of the one single promise I've ever made to him and how close I am to breaking it.

He didn't want me to get involved with his friends at all. Even though he doesn't know that I'm only here until June, it was still important enough for him to bring up, knowing it could cause lasting complications in his friendship with them.

These next few months are barely going to be enough time to solidify our relationship as siblings, let alone adding in convincing him that it's okay for me to get involved with one of his best friends.

And that's my reason, I decide, for keeping my distance from Ethan.

With that resolve at the forefront of my mind, I continue on. I'm almost surprised at how quickly the next month moves forward—the weeks fly by as I settle more into this version of normalcy here.

During the week, I still do homework with Ethan—

although it's a little awkward at first—while Caleb and Benjamin either play games or study with us.

I hang out with the girls almost every Saturday night, usually at Brooke's house but occasionally at Sophia's.

I put all the notes I get from Heidi in a drawer and even spend an entire Saturday with her at a salon, watching firsthand how she keeps her blonde hair so perfect.

Trey and I keep up our morning routine, and eventually, we start to have conversations that aren't strictly related to tea or crossword puzzles.

On Thanksgiving morning, though, I wake tangled in the sheets, completely unsettled after endless nightmares.

It was the most vivid recollection of the accident yet, revealing some of those parts I blocked out, like the very vivid memory of my mother's lifeless eyes and all the blood in the car.

It shakes me so hard to my core I skip breakfast and the daily crossword, choosing to sit in the bathtub fully clothed while trying to find my composure.

"Avery?" Heidi calls, knocking on my bathroom door.

I should have made sure to lock my bedroom door as well, keeping her far away, but at least she knows I'm alive, just hiding or sick.

"Are you okay in there?"

Her voice has an increasing tinge of panic in it, and it's only a matter of time before she finds some way to pick the lock or break down the door completely.

"Yeah," I call back, but my voice is hoarse.

"Are you sure?"

I can picture the frown on her face, marring her beautiful and otherwise flawless features.

"Yeah." My voice is more resolute this time.

"The Navarros are coming up for dinner in an hour. If you want to get ready, I got you a little Thanksgiving gift while shopping last weekend."

I close my eyes and press my palms to my face.

Why does Heidi have to be so nice and thoughtful?

If she were less, I could hide in here forever without a second thought.

When I hear my bedroom door shut, I sigh and stand, numbly working through my getting ready process of showering, styling my hair, and doing my makeup.

I stare at the thin pink line of my scar exposed while I hover over my cheek with the brush I just used to cover up the dark circles under my eyes, but for some reason I can't find one good reason why I should cover it up.

So I don't.

The dress Heidi picked is, of course, beautiful.

It's olive green and has a vintage feel, with a v-neck, buttons down the front, and squared sleeves. Knowing my unease with heels, she paired it with black pointed flats.

If I let her, Heidi would dress me up like a doll every single day.

And maybe I should.

As I'm smoothing on a light shade of lipstick, I hear the Navarros come through the front door and head into the living room.

Not wanting to be wrangled by Heidi again, I open the door to go introduce myself, but I bump right into Ethan's chest.

"Sorry," I say, stepping back.

I haven't been up close and personal—or alone—with

him since the club. I'm very nervous to be in his presence, mostly because I'm still shaken up by last night but also because I don't know how to handle him or this feeling inside me.

His eyes take me in appreciatively until he catches my expression.

"You okay?" Ethan asks.

I chew on my bottom lip while I nod.

"Heidi asked me to come collect you," he says, holding out a hand for me.

I think it's a friendly gesture, one I shouldn't read too much into, but I soften at the contact, just like I did when he first took my hand in Central Park.

As we approach the others, he drops my hand in favor of putting it on my back, like he knows I need the reassurance.

Mr. and Mrs. Navarro are very polite and a little rigid, greeting me as we sit down at the table. They smile kindly at me before they reengage their conversation with Heidi and Trey, pretending as if the rest of us don't exist.

They name drop endlessly, drink a fair share of wine, and talk about business and extravagant purchases they've made.

I learn that somehow, the Navarros and Carters are connected through business deals in the medical manufacturing industry and that Mr. Navarro went to college with Trey.

I wonder if he was there the night my mom got pregnant, but I don't dare vocalize that question.

As Benjamin scoops his third helping of mashed potatoes onto his plate, I have a revelation.

The Navarros personify the expectations I set for Heidi and Trey—cold and distant rich people who treat their children as if they're not worth much—and I don't understand how these distinct personality types can find friendship.

But then again, Ethan and I are pretty much the opposites of our siblings, and we all get along well enough.

"Trey tells me you're looking at a career in the medical field, Avery," Mr. Navarro says, finally addressing me directly.

"Yes," I admit. "That's what I'm hoping for, anyway."

"We're going to spend the day together at the hospital tomorrow," Trey tells him proudly. "She's going to shadow a few departments to get a feel for the different workloads and experiences."

"Isn't that nice?" Mrs. Navarro hums.

Heidi smiles at her over a glass of wine. "We're very proud."

They have no reason to be proud of me, really.

With no hand in my upbringing other than the last few months and a little kindness aside, it's not like they have claim to something I've been interested in pursuing for years.

I sigh, annoyed at myself for being mentally snippy and ungrateful, but I just can't shake it off today.

"Maybe she should come by the lab next," Mr. Navarro suggests. "Maybe hospital life isn't for her."

"Maybe she and I will decide to both go into private practice and open up a shop together," Caleb says.

"Maybe she could speak for herself after tomorrow and get back to you," Heidi cuts in, earning a polite laugh around the table.

"It's just reassuring to hear that there's some direction happening," Mr. Navarro says. "With Benjamin's interest in architecture and these two going into the family business —" I pale at that line. "—all that we have left is Ethan to get accounted for, and we're all set."

Ethan's expression pinches, and his interest in cutting up his turkey renews significantly.

"How one of our boys has such drive and grades and the other is faltering so spectacularly, I'll never know," Mrs. Navarro says in disapproval.

When I first met the Navarro parents, I was a little nervous, intimidated even. I fiddled with the hem of my dress and was glad that they mostly ignored me, but now, I can't seem to care less about making a good impression.

Sure, they're friends of Heidi and Trey, but from everything I know about them, they certainly can't be down with this treatment.

So why aren't they saying something?

Almost every eye in the room glazes over, like this is the same topic of conversation that has come up again and again, but this is the first time I'm going to hear it—and the last.

"I think Ethan is more the standard than all of us," I say. "What kind of insane person has their entire life figured out during their senior year of high school?"

Ethan looks at me gratefully, but still tentatively, while his father narrows his eyes in my direction like I betrayed whatever opinion of me he formed in his mind.

"A person who is going far in life," Mr. Navarro says abruptly. "Not someone who is content to coast while chasing some liberal arts degree. To be successful, you need direction and a way to do it."

"Well, until two months ago, I was with my very much alive mother and planning on scraping by for nursing school, and now I'm here, so you'd be surprised how things can change," I warn. "Try not to take it all for granted. Sometimes life gets out of control, but it can work out, if you let it."

The Navarro parents both flush red, but everyone else looks at me with...a mixture of surprise and pride.

It's the most I've spoken aloud at once to anyone in months, and I've put my stake in the ground of what I won't stand for when it comes to the people I care about.

It's long overdue—both the stake in the ground and the admitting that I care.

"Martha," Heidi calls. "I think we're ready for dessert."

The rest of our time in the dining room is tense, and nearly the entire conversation is focused on the food itself. But rightfully so—it's some of the best pumpkin pie I've had in my entire life.

The parents all excuse themselves, off to have coffee in Trey's office and combat the turkey's tryptophan, while the boys and I still pick at desserts.

Caleb speaks first. "That. Was. Awesome. Epic Five!"

It really wasn't that impressive of a speech, but I think he's referring to the intention, not the actual words themselves.

Still, I hold up my hand so he can smack it with his.

"So awesome," Benjamin confirms, shooting a spray from the can of whipped cream into his mouth.

Ethan doesn't hide his smile. "Definitely makes up for

the fact that you've been sitting in my seat since you got here."

"Your seat?" I balk, briefly glancing down at my lap.

"My seat," he says. "I didn't want to say anything because...well, I just didn't want to. But now, I feel like the truth can come out."

I glance at Caleb, seated beside me, and realize that I am, in fact, disrupting the flow between families at the table. I didn't notice it with the small group, but it makes sense that the Carters sit at one end and the Navarros at the other.

I took his seat and the room above his.

My mind wants to think it means something, but some part of rationality prevails, and I decide I absolutely need to stop creating these false intimacies.

I find comfort in the realization that at least I'm not as bad as Benjamin, pining after someone he can barely speak to—or maybe we're both delusional.

"So what do you want to do?" Benjamin asks Ethan. "After you graduate high school, I mean. Not with the whole seating arrangement thing. I think we're stuck with that for now."

"I still don't know," Ethan admits.

"You really don't have any idea?" Caleb asks, trying to keep his voice as light as possible.

The question still earns him a glare from his brother. "Okay, Dr. Navarro," he says.

Caleb rolls his eyes in response.

"You like to write and read, future Shakespeare," I remind him. "Plenty of jobs involving those two things."

Ethan's gaze flicks over to me, watching me fiddle with

the end of the fork before he clears his throat. "I also enjoy talking to people...and I don't hate the idea of doing something to help out. I don't know. I'm sure that our mother would love it if I went into something like corporate charity work, but it just seems so..."

"Soul crushing?" Caleb says at the same time Benjamin says, "Boring?"

I sigh, wondering if the reason Ethan doesn't have direction, Caleb is stuck in the longest text-fight known to humankind, and Benjamin is absolutely clueless is because they're all useless in trying to give one another advice.

Whatever the reason, I'm here now, shields lowering and emotions at the ready.

"I'm sure we can figure out something," I say before I scoop up the last dollop of whipped cream from my plate.

FOURTEEN

"It looks like Christmas exploded in here," Trey says.

He glances around the kitchen and living room, taking in the disarray.

Somehow, the apartment turned into Santa's workshop overnight.

There are boxes overflowing with Christmas decorations, some of which have already been placed around the room, but everything is overshadowed by a massive artificial tree that holds a few ornaments on its branches.

"You know Heidi," Martha says. "Always likes to start on the holidays early."

"Probably for the best that we're heading out today," Trey mutters, pouring hot water over the tea bag in his to-go cup.

"Are you sure I can't get you anything?" Martha asks me. "Tea? Toast? Granola bar?"

"No, thank you," I tell her.

We're up earlier than usual so we can get to the hospital

before the next shift starts, but that's not why I'm not hungry.

The truth is that I'm too anxious to eat anything right now. I'm both nervous and excited to spend the day with my father—and shadow the staff at Carter-Churchill Medical.

"Car's here," Trey announces.

Even though the Carters have a car of their own in the underground garage, Trey uses a car service to take him to and from work every day, claiming it's far less of a hassle.

If it were nicer weather, I would suggest a walk, but it's cold enough that I tug my winter jacket around me as I dash from the lobby to the door of the black SUV.

It's the same one I rode in after the accident, and although I've changed since then, I'm still marveled by watching us zoom past the stores and the people. But Trey, having done this ride thousands of times, goes through emails on his phone.

When we arrive, he whisks me through the employees-only entrance with a swipe of his keycard, and I feel like a VIP being ushered through the automatic doors.

I think you can tell a lot about a person by the way they are received by their peers and employees, even just casually with a morning hello.

Like at the restaurant, the general manager is so rude and widely feared that everyone averts their eyes and busies themselves whenever he shows up for a shift. If he happens to make an appearance during the dead zone hours in the middle of the day, we all keep a list of things to do in order to avoid contact with him.

Even though Trey has the fancy "Chairman and CEO"

title, I'm pleased to see that every single person we pass on the way up to his office enthusiastically smiles and waves in his direction—even the folks gripping coffee cups and wiping away the tiredness from their eyes.

"Because of the holiday weekend, I don't have any meetings for you to sit in on," Trey says, shrugging out of his overcoat once we reach his office.

He looks every bit the part of his title—tailored suit, hair slicked back, expensive watch on his wrist.

I glance at my own outfit, realizing that in my dark gray dress I look more like him now than a girl who works in a restaurant in Pennsylvania. Every single item I'm wearing has a brand name, all the way up to the earrings Heidi insisted I needed.

Had I planned on staying here long-term, or was even considering working in the hospital, I probably would have tried to dress down—I wouldn't need people to see me waltzing around like I'm a shoe-in for a job here because of nepotism instead of merit.

But at the moment, I don't mind blending in with Trey, especially as he makes dozens of introductions throughout the morning, giving me the official tour of the hospital.

He fills me in on the details of the history, how they've invested more in research and trials in partnership with the Navarros, and his vision for the future.

I ask every single question that surfaces, wanting to understand as much as I can about running a hospital and how the mechanics of it actually work.

I'm impressed by Trey's enthusiasm about employee retention and some programs they've created to improve the mental health of employees, especially those "on the front lines."

"But every single person here is crucial to how we operate," Trey explains. "Those who clean and sanitize ORs are just as important as the people operating within it. It's a delicate balance, but I try to have as much transparency as I can with the staff, so they understand why we're investing in personnel in some places while cutting back on new equipment orders in others."

"How did you...figure out how to do all this?" I ask him.

I understand that a college degree can help with theory, and even give practical experience sometimes, but it seems like this behavior isn't something one can learn in a classroom.

"Just like you are figuring things out," he says easily as we observe an appendectomy through a window.

"What do you mean?"

"My father...your grandfather...was a brilliant surgeon, but he had no business acumen or interest. That was all my mother. She was the first person on her side of the family to go to college, and she had dreams with even bigger dollar signs."

I guess I don't mind the idea of sharing a gene pool with smart, successful people.

"Of course, she never really got the chance to 'make it' in the New York business market, but she was all too happy to give me free advice when my first medical start-up went public," he explains. "That's how, eventually, I bought the hospital."

"Why this?" I ask. "Why a hospital and not some other venture?"

He crosses his arms, and although his gaze fixes through the glass, I can tell he's staring at the memory, not necessarily at the patient.

"It's the place where my dad found out he had incurable cancer and my mother died of a heart attack a year later." He pauses. "That's a little dark, I know, but it's also where Benjamin and I were both born, and where I proposed to Heidi after said birth—"

"What?" I balk.

He laughs as he gestures for me to follow him back out into the hall. "Yes, you heard me correctly. We ended up eloping a while later, but given how colicky Benjamin was, part of me expected her to run far, far away from us Carter boys and never look back."

It's funny to think about them being a young couple with a newborn, figuring out how to make their careers and lives work, instead of the powerhouse they are together now.

Trey brings us to a stop in front of two double doors. "Are you okay with seeing the ER?" he asks tentatively.

In all the shows I watch, the ER is where the most drama occurs. It's frantic, fast-paced, and there's always someone inconsolable. I don't mind a little blood, even if it's from an—

I stop as the realization hits.

Trey is concerned it will give me horrible flashbacks to my own accident.

In fact, I probably should be worried about it, too, but I'm not. I mean, if I really want to make it in the medical industry, this is an excellent litmus test to see how I handle it.

"Yes, I'm okay," I say, full of confidence I don't know I have buried in me.

He nods resolutely and pushes the doors open.

Of course, it's chaos, but not as much as I expected. More like, it's just busy and not exactly the all-out panic drama I see portrayed by actors.

Trey has arranged for us to shadow a woman named Dr. Michaels, and while I would probably falter under such scrutiny, she seems enthusiastic to have us following her around.

She gives me the quick rundown of how the ER is set up, then it's time for her to start checking in on patients.

I take special notes of the process she uses—the careful tone and neutral face as she listens to concerns, checks stitches, and makes notes in their charts.

As we linger outside a semi-private patient room, Trey's phone buzzes loudly in his pocket.

"Sorry, it's Heidi," he says, stepping away to take the call.

I watch as Dr. Michaels finishes evaluating a set of burn marks on the patient's hand, which are the result of attempting to deep-fry a turkey yesterday, and promises to send in a nurse in her place shortly.

"So what do you think?" Dr. Michaels asks, leading me back toward the nurse's station.

"He is very lucky," I say with a frown.

She laughs. "Yes, but I meant about the hospital itself, maybe even emergency medicine."

I glance around at all the people in their beds. "It's…"

Most are sleeping or resting, some are visibly in pain, a

few are chatting with nurses, and at least one is trying to swindle some additional pain medicine their way.

These people seem stable for now, like there's a good chance they're going to get out of here just fine after some rest and pills, but not everyone gets to be that lucky. This is what Trey was concerned about—the onslaught of emotion in his place of business.

But I think to become a health professional, I have to have some sort of insatiable need to help people and want the best for them, and I think I do have it. Like how, even though I pulled up my defenses and suppressed all my outward emotions, I've been feeling everything.

Tenderness for Heidi. Appreciation for Trey. Friendship for Caleb, Brooke, and Sophia. Something like lust for Ethan. And protection for Benjamin.

And still, I've continued on.

I couldn't protect my mother, and I won't be able to protect every single patient. I'm going to have to deal with traumas all over again if this is what I pursue, but maybe I can use my own experience to become more relatable. After all, there's an endless stream of people who need help—but I'm sure it's mentally taxing in ways that I can't even begin to imagine yet.

"There you both are," Trey says.

I realize I haven't responded to Dr. Michaels, who has been eyeing me as I've been mulling everything over in my mind.

Something in the look she gives me says she understands how my mind has been processing everything, but maybe I'm reading too much into it.

"We'll get out of your hair, Carrie," Trey says. "Thank you again for letting us follow along."

"Of course," she returns with a smile. "Avery, it was lovely to meet you. I hope to see you back here again someday."

"Thank you," I tell her, surprising myself when I add, "Me too."

Trey beams at that, then ushers me over toward the elevators.

"Do you want to go out for lunch?" he asks me.

"Isn't there a cafeteria in this building?"

"Yes, but..." He pauses, almost as if he's surprised that I don't want to go out to some fancy restaurant. "Sure, let's go there."

I'm happy to have the employee lunch experience. Hospital food is notoriously bland, but this is actually great.

Trey mentions it's part of ensuring a healthy workplace for employees to not have to sprint out during their breaks for something other than sandwiches and vending machine snacks.

I select a chicken piccata that's on top of an enormous bed of greens, knowing my mother would be excited for the number of vitamins and minerals I'm consuming at once, even if I'm mostly focused on consuming all the parmesan cheese.

"So," Trey says, clearing his throat. "There's a big hospital fundraiser in two weeks."

I know this because there are papers on every bulletin board of the hospital, but I nod, somewhat disinterested.

"All the staff who aren't on shifts are invited, and it's a

big fancy, black-tie to-do. It's our biggest event of the year. Last year we ended up funding a dozen pro-bono heart surgeries in our pediatrics center, but I'm hoping to beat it by a mile this year."

"That's great," I say, trying to wrangle a piece of kale into a manageable bite.

"Would you want to go?" Trey asks. "I have to give a big opening speech, and...there's a spot for you at the family table, if you'd want it."

He's not just asking me to dress up. He's pressing for something deeper.

Today was a test of sorts—maybe not intentionally, but it was an opportunity to feel each other out without the safety of Heidi and Benjamin, and I think we both found some common ground that doesn't feel too stiff or forced.

And now he's trying to move us right along.

I don't mind it all that much. "Sure," I say. "Sounds cool."

"Cool," he repeats, and it sounds funny coming from a man in a thousand-dollar suit.

He laughs because he knows how ridiculous it sounds, and I feel my facial muscles moving in ways they haven't since the day of the accident.

Trey watches the tentative chuckle spread across my face with wide eyes, like he's witnessing a miracle, then he blinks and collects himself, not wanting to draw attention to the obvious.

"After we finish up here, the boys and I are going to wrangle a tree for us to decorate tonight," Trey says, changing the subject. "I think we passed a few vendors on the street getting ready to sell for the season."

"But wasn't there a fake tree in the process of being decorated when we left this morning?" I ask.

He laughs. "Oh, there are *multiple* trees. It's Christmas, after all."

I shake my head. "Right. Of course."

FIFTEEN

"Are Sophia and Caleb fighting again?" Brooke asks.

"When are they not fighting?" I deadpan, then follow her gaze.

I turn to look over my shoulder, seeing that they've completely abandoned the worksheet in front of them.

Usually, they bicker without breaking the stride of their work, which means this is an entirely new level of arguing that I haven't witnessed before.

"Caleb looks upset," Brooke says. "This must be the phase where Sophia realizes she made a mistake and wants to get him back."

"It's really that predictable of a cycle?"

"Oh, yeah. It's a weird circle of codependency. They won't listen to anyone. I try my best to stay out of it, but it's hard to do when Sophia is in denial, and Caleb looks legitimately upset."

I spare another quick glance in his direction, noticing the hard line of his jaw and the tears surfacing in her eyes.

When he catches my gaze, it's with complete sadness, and I feel for him. Caleb is usually so full of life, telling jokes at Ethan's expense, and I don't enjoy seeing him like this.

Caleb and Sophia pointedly ignore each other for the rest of the day, making for a somewhat awkward lunch. I internally argue with myself all day on whether to get involved.

It's not really my place to interfere, but going back to my thoughts on Thanksgiving, when I realized these three teenage boys are hopeless in helping one another, I can't stop myself from caring.

I force myself not to overthink it as I knock on the front door of the Navarro apartment after school, hoping that neither of the parents opens the door.

I breathe a sigh of relief when it's Caleb.

"Avery," he says, and his face immediately brightens at my unexpected visit. "Hey."

"Hey," I return.

We stand there, me nervously shuffling between my feet and him hanging in the doorway, until he remembers himself.

"Come in," he offers, stepping aside for me to do so.

I've only been inside once, briefly, before school to collect the boys a few weeks ago so we could walk together. It was long enough to see the red paint color Benjamin mentioned but not much else. Now, with a little more time to adjust, I can see the vastly different decorating style between Heidi and Mrs. Navarro.

Caleb leads me down to the kitchen, and I frown at Ethan's closed door.

Although I'm here for a very specific purpose—to check in on Caleb—I wouldn't be upset if I got a look into Ethan's room. I think it's kind of intimate, like getting a personal glimpse into someone's mind, especially considering that he sleeps just a floor away from me. I wonder if his bed is in the same spot as mine or if he stares at the ceiling when he falls asleep.

"So, what can I do for you, Miss Miller?" Caleb asks, interrupting my inappropriate line of thinking.

"I just wanted to make sure you're okay." When he gives me a blank look, I add, "Brooke noticed you and Sophia were arguing in class—"

"*Brooke* was concerned?" There's a lightness in his eyes that I appreciate.

I sigh. "Okay, I'm totally not trying to be the prying sister type, but I guess I can't help it."

He laughs and leans on the countertop. "I don't mind it," he admits. "Actually, I think it's kind of cute."

"No girl wants to be called 'cute,' Caleb. Even by a very platonic—" Another vocabulary word. "—friend."

"Normally I would tell you that I very much do not need advice in the girl department, but as you can see, I'm not exactly doing great these days."

"Do you want to talk about it?" I ask him. "Or do you want to watch some *Scrubs* episodes and watch nine seasons of dysfunctional J.D. and Elliott to make yourself feel better?"

He pretends to consider it with very deep thought, tapping a finger on his chin before he says, "I think I'll take door number two."

"Excellent Choice Five," I say, holding up my hand.

We slap hands, then he leaves me to cue up the episode of my choice while he makes popcorn.

I scroll through the list of episodes before deciding on one of my favorites just in time for him to jump over the back of the couch, somehow managing to not spill a single kernel.

"Season three, huh?"

"The best."

He frowns. "Season five has it beat."

"No way," I argue. "Carla and Turk get married in this episode."

"But the entire storyline with J.D., Elliott, and Sean is so annoying."

I hit the play button, not bothering to spell out the parallels of watching two people repeatedly argue, dragging their friends down along with it.

We watch a few episodes, and I slowly get more comfortable, enjoying the familiarity of the jokes and the way Caleb snorts a little when he laughs at them.

Part of me is relieved that Caleb didn't want to go in depth on his relationship troubles with Sophia because it's really nice to just sit and enjoy something together. I'm also honestly not too sure how helpful I would be in handing out advice, but I know it's just nice to sit and relax in the presence of someone who cares about you.

"I know about you and Ethan," Caleb says after what must be the sixth episode we've watched together.

I blink, startled by the sound of his voice and the words out of his mouth. "What?"

He smiles at me. "Call it a twin thing, call it intuition,

call it seeing you both going at each other on Halloween," he says nonchalantly.

"Oh god," I groan, clutching a pillow to my chest.

"Don't worry, though, Benjamin didn't see. I ran interference for you."

"And you're just telling me this now?"

"Well, I thought it might have just been a one-time thing, but since you verbally stabbed my father on Thanksgiving, I've noticed all the weird staring and pining you two have going on." He chuckles at his own description. "And if you're planning to do anything more than that, you should probably tell Ben sooner rather than later."

I'm equal parts grateful and mortified he brought up the topic—and even more so when he goes back to watching one of Dr. Cox's rants like he didn't just throw a grenade in my lap.

On a basic level, I understand that my own brother would want to be aware of what's happening in my personal life.

I think it's a little childish that he's so territorial over his friends, even if they got into that big fight that ruined their eighth grade dance.

I'm also not sure how I would even approach him to tell him I kissed his best friend only to spend the month following in a strange abyss, existing in the same spaces but not really acknowledging each other or what happened.

I sigh and sink back into the cushion, trying to get lost in the show once again, but my mind can't seem to break away from thoughts of Ethan.

"Well, I think I'll go upstairs to keep Sir Benjamin company," Caleb says as the next set of credits roll.

"Oh, I'll get out—"

Caleb cuts me off. "Mom and Dad are out tonight, so you're on your own for dinner."

I spin, realizing he said the words to Ethan, who is leaning against the wall that separates the living room from the kitchen and has been there for who knows how long.

"Stay safe, kids," Caleb calls as he walks down the hall and lets the front door slam behind him.

Ethan moves first, but it's not to me—it's toward the doors of the terrace.

Even without a direct invitation, I follow him without hesitation.

"See, I told you this isn't as nice as yours," he says, sticking his hands in his pockets and walking over toward the ledge.

I glance around, noticing the smaller size and slightly obstructed view.

Despite his bad-mouthing, I don't let that deter me from appreciating the beauty.

I rest my arms on the ledge, taking in the lights and allure of New York.

It's not just the beautiful buildings or the sounds in the distance that intrigue me, it's that even on a weeknight in the middle of December, this city feels alive.

I should feel overwhelmed or even small, standing here and witnessing this view, but I feel enveloped in the city itself, a part of something that's bigger than me. I'm one person in the city of millions, and my struggles are one of many.

"'The skies are painted with unnumbered sparks,'"

Ethan murmurs. "'They are all fire and everyone doth shine.'"

I hum. "You really do have a Shakespeare quote for every situation."

"Yeah, well, it would probably be more romantic if there was no light pollution and we could actually see the stars," he says lightly.

The breeze picks up, gently moving the ends of my hair, and I shiver.

Ethan slips off his jacket and puts it around my shoulders, enveloping me in the scent of leather and citrus.

"Are you trying to be romantic?" I ask him.

He bites back a grin before it spreads completely. "If you're even asking that question, I think I'm failing."

Lightness bubbles up inside me, and I reach for his hand, breaking the standoff that's been between us since we were wound up in each other's arms on the dance floor.

His hand, warm and rough, still fits perfectly with mine.

"Did you hear what Caleb said to me?" I ask him.

He sighs. "If it makes you feel better, he's given me a similar speech many times since that night."

"So you've talked to your brother more about what happened than you have the other person involved in said nameless event who you have been ignoring?" I pose. "How very capricious of you."

There's a vertical line that forms between his eyebrows when he's concentrating.

I've seen it a dozen times while doing homework together, and I see it now as he's trying to recall the definition of one of the vocabulary words that didn't actually make an appearance on the SAT for me.

"Sudden change of mood," I prompt.

He frowns. "I don't think I want to be associated with that one. I just figured you'd want some time to process everything."

"Well, I think I'm done," I say, watching the line deepen once again. "Processing, I mean."

He squeezes my hand. "Good."

"What's this from?" I ask, tracing a little white scar on his thumb.

"I don't even remember," he admits.

I smile at that admission, and he gasps at the sight.

"Shit," he says, blue eyes round and startled.

I pull back on instinct and in confusion, but he renews his hold, forcing me even closer to him.

"I, uh, don't think I've ever seen you smile before," he clarifies.

The muscles on my face that hold it in place are practically atrophied at this point, so it falls off my face just as quickly as it surfaced.

"You're absolutely stunning, Avery," he says, tilting my chin upward so our gazes meet. "I know every woman ever hates this phrase, but...you should *definitely* smile more."

I place my hand on his chest, right on his scar, and once again acquaint myself with the rhythm of his pounding heart.

"I'm working on it," I tell him, inching even closer to him.

My eyelids flutter shut, expecting the feel of his lips on mine, but he presses kisses from my jaw to my temple, right along the line of the scar.

"'Go, girl, seek happy nights to happy days,'" he whispers, then captures my lips with his.

In the weeks that follow, this becomes a habit between Ethan and me.

All the Shakespeare quoting, kissing, and scar-touching.

We're acknowledging the permanent marks on each other, and I'm slightly terrified he's going to be one of those, too, just hidden beneath layers of emotion instead of on my skin for everyone else to see.

Ethan and I meet in secret between classes or sneak off when Benjamin and Caleb are preoccupied, but it's a rarity, given that we're an established foursome.

Around the others, we keep our distance from each other.

I'm not ready for the scrutiny and gossip, and I think it would shift the easy dynamic between all of us into something uncomfortable.

Plus, we haven't defined anything, given a name or acknowledgment to the feelings growing between us, and until then, I'm not sure if it's worth even bringing up.

The week before Christmas, Trey and Heidi are out all day doing a wine tasting and vineyard tour somewhere in New Jersey, and I've actually wrangled Benjamin into being productive.

For him, it's writing an essay, but for me, it's slightly panicking over college applications and reading the fine print of scholarship requirements to make sure I'm still eligible for ones to Pennsylvania schools even though I technically do not live there.

Trey and Heidi have been covering rent on the apartment my mother and I shared. I only agreed to this—and their covering of the medical bills—until the insurance money comes through from the accident and I can repay them.

Which means I'll have much less than I hoped for to get on my feet.

"What's that?" Benjamin asks.

"Scholarship applications," I answer plainly. "And financial aid forms."

And unfortunately, the costs for community college and small universities here are astronomically higher than Pennsylvania, so if I wanted to stay, I can't afford to do so. And that's calculating the possibility of Heidi and Trey letting me stay here, but even then, everything else will be too much.

"What do you need those for?" he asks, genuinely confused.

I level with him. "Because I'm poor."

He bursts out laughing. "You're joking."

"Do you need me to show you my bank account?"

"You think Mom and Dad are going to let you put any sort of financial strain on yourself now that you're here? Or because of pride or whatever? You're crazy."

"I can't just show up out of nowhere and allow them to do all this for me, Benjamin. The clothes, the electronics, the healthcare...it's all more than I could have ever asked for—"

"Those are actually just basic things people need to live in this decade, little sis."

"I don't need you to patronize me," I tell him. "Or remind me how I can't even afford the bare minimum."

He takes off Caleb's borrowed glasses so he can glare at

me more effectively. "I can't even argue with you on this because it's so absurd."

I've seen so many emotions on Benjamin's features these past few months, but I've never seen this level of frustration and anger.

It brings me to a complete loss of words.

The front door opens, and the sound of Caleb and Ethan's laughter is a stark contrast to the quiet standoff Benjamin and I are having.

"What's going on?" Ethan asks, sensing the tension they both walked into.

I give Benjamin my best pleading look to keep his mouth shut.

"Nothing," Benjamin sighs.

"Good, because we brought Shake Shack," Caleb says proudly, dropping two bags on the table.

My brother is practically salivating at the smell, and the heaviness of our conversation seems to disappear in his mind in favor of his excitement.

"Did you get me a double? With a black and white shake? And chicken bites?"

"We got it all."

I wish I got Benjamin's metabolism in the gene pool, but it's impressive to watch him consume massive numbers of calories in one sitting.

"Weren't sure what you liked, so we went with the classics," Ethan says, sliding a wrapped burger, box of fries, and vanilla shake my direction.

"Perfect," I say. "Thank you. Did they give ketchup?"

He jokingly dumps the entire collection from the bag

out, but he's baffled when I tear open multiple packets at once. "That's an ungodly amount of ketchup, Avery."

"And what exactly is a godly amount of ketchup?" I ask. "So I know for future reference."

Ethan takes in the growing pile of wrappers. "Whatever it is, it's less than that."

I roll my eyes. "I'm from Pittsburgh, the Heinz Ketchup capital of the world. It's, like, a requirement I use ketchup on everything."

"Everything?"

"Well, not everything, but most potato products."

"Potato chips?" Benjamin asks.

"Of course," I say. "It's just like eating them with french fries. All that salty fatty goodness."

Benjamin pretends to gag. "Gross."

"Yeah, but you're not going to eat it with mashed potatoes," Ethan argues.

That actually sounds pretty disgusting, but I hold my ground. "Says who?"

"Says you, who didn't use an ounce of ketchup on Thanksgiving."

"Touché."

SIXTEEN

Even when I'm not around him, I swear I can *feel* Ethan.

I constantly replay our interactions—him jotting down Shakespeare quotes on the margins of my English notebook, asking for my opinions on everything from favorite foods and music to politics and philosophy while we walk to school, and helping Trey and me finish the crossword puzzle at breakfast.

It's worse at night when I think about how he's a floor away.

In the silence and darkness, I give myself permission to blush at the way he makes me feel when he touches me, and I wonder if he's doing the same thing.

It's lunacy, but it's part of the new me.

And when we're in the same room, it's clear—to me, at least—that there's something between us. There's an invisible tether pulling me to him, and I'm getting more bold at the thought of holding onto it.

I don't think anyone has caught on yet, but it might only be a matter of time.

On the last day of school before winter break, Brooke asks me to go for coffee after school.

We have spent enough time together that it's a normal thing for her to ask, but with all the Ethan thoughts swirling in my mind, I'm nervous that she has picked up on something, and I spend the rest of the day worrying about what exactly to say.

"Are you even in the mood for coffee?" Brooke asks, meeting up with me after the last bell rings.

"Not really." I'm never actually in the mood to drink anything other than Trey's favorite mint tea.

"How do you feel about going on a walk and eating some vegan food?"

"Sure," I say. "Still not recovered from carving up the frog, huh?"

She laughs before her expression shifts to a grimace. "That was the start of it, but then I went down this spiral of videos and documentaries. It's gotten even worse since then, and let me tell you, cheese without dairy in it is an acquired taste."

"Weren't you just trying to talk me into going to a vegan restaurant?" I tease.

"This will be worth it, I promise you."

As we walk, she points out various landmarks and tells me more about her experiences growing up here, going on field trips to museums and sneaking out to go see midnight releases at the movie theater nearby.

When we get to Candle Cafe, a cute little restaurant that ironically sits between a steakhouse and butcher shop,

I sigh in relief at how good the food looks that some of the patrons are eating.

We sit, and Brooke takes charge, ordering us fresh juices and a few appetizers to split.

Our conversation mostly consists of small talk about school—classmates, homework, college applications—but it doesn't feel forced.

"This is actually perfect," I tell Brooke as the server drops off our juices. "Heidi is already talking about all the Christmas cookies and pies she wants us to bake together. All these fruits and vegetables will cancel it out, right? No exercise required?"

She laughs. "Definitely. At least that's what I'm going to tell myself because I've tried to be one of those people who loves running, and let me tell you, it just isn't working."

"I can relate," I say, swirling the green liquid around in the glass before I take a sip. "I'm not too athletically inclined."

Last spring, my mom got into a weird fitness kick, saying that it'd be good for us to do a better job taking care of ourselves. We tried running and at-home yoga videos, but the only thing that stuck long term was her incessant need to get me to eat more vegetables.

"Aren't you some sort of air hockey prodigy?" Brooke asks me.

I eye her. "Where did you hear that?"

"Sophia was complaining about it," she says. "Apparently after you guys went to Coney Island, it was all Caleb and Ethan could talk about for days."

"Oh, well, I don't really count air hockey as athleticism.

Just strategy, reflexes, and catching your opponent by surprise."

"Noted." She laughs and shuffles our drinks, making room for the plates of food our server drops off, then picks at the little pieces of soy steak that are in the quesadilla she ordered, even though it's still hot from the kitchen.

"So," I decide to cut right to it, "was there something you wanted to talk to me about?"

"What do you mean?"

"I assumed you asked me to go out because you had something you wanted to discuss?"

She gives me a look of complete amusement. "I just wanted to hang out."

I breathe a sigh of relief. "Good."

"No ulterior motive," she insists. "That would be a very Sophia thing to do, though. One time she insisted we get our hair done together because it would be 'fun,' only for it to come out that she booked me an eyebrow wax because she disapproved of how I was shaping mine."

"Wow." I self-consciously run my finger over my eyebrow, then down my cheek, over my scar. "Can't imagine what she had to say about this when I first arrived."

That sobers Brooke up immediately.

She prematurely swallows a bite of her food and chases it down with a big gulp of juice.

"I've actually wanted to talk to you about that...I know that we're friends now and all that, but I never really apologized for what I said on the first day."

I'm trying to remember what happened on the first day that she felt the need to apologize for, but I draw a blank.

"Insulting Benjamin," she prompts, and it sounds vaguely familiar. "When I found out you two were related, it kind of threw me."

"Oh," I say, waving her off. "Don't worry about that."

"It's just you're so...different," she continues. "In a good way. I mean, every single time he talks to me, he insults me."

I blink rapidly. "What? How?"

Brooke puts on a deep, mocking tone. "'Oh, do you drink iced coffee all year, then? Do you not wear skirts because you find them uncomfortable or you don't like how they look? You're not wearing as much makeup today, are you? You got a B on that paper?'"

She laughs, and I frown.

My protective instincts kick in, and it's not necessarily to defend him but to save him from himself.

"Brooke," I say slowly. "He has it so bad for you, I'm actually very surprised he has managed to form complete sentences around you."

That stops her. "He...what?"

"He's crazy about you. In the 'holy crap I will never live up to this woman's expectations of me' kind of way, so he's just a nervous, bumbling idiot around you," I tell her. "But he means well. Notices all the little things like when you get a new pair of shoes or are having an off day and forces me to make sure you're okay. Hell, the Navarros' dining room is painted the exact same shade as your red hair because Benjamin wouldn't shut up about how it was the most magnificent color in all the swatches."

I stop myself because I think I've said too much, but the

very definite surprise and smugness that's overtaking her face confirms that I've done us all a favor.

She's speechless for a moment, so I pick at the mezze platter while she sifts through her thoughts.

Eventually, she clears her throat. "Did you know that your dad's hospital is having a big fundraiser?"

This is a surprising turn in the conversation.

"Yeah," I say.

"Well, Sophia has been talking about it for weeks because she found the perfect dress—"

"Sophia's going?"

"With Caleb. They agreed when they were still together, and she's 'not going to give up a night of possibly finding a doctor husband' just because she has to go with her ex-boyfriend."

I hide my snort by taking a sip of green juice.

"I was wondering...do you think it would be weird to ask Benjamin myself? I mean, I'm all for grand romantic gestures, but because I've known him for years but didn't know...it just seems like a good way to show my intentions."

"Well, if it's your intentions—"

"Oh, shut up," Brooke says with a laugh.

"You are talking about my brother, don't forget."

"Yes, your very fidgety, tall, and hot brother."

I wrinkle my nose, but of course I'll do anything to help. "Let's get the check and head back to my place," I say. "We can get these plans solidified tonight, and then you can pay back Sophia and go on your own quest of finding the perfect dress."

We pay and hurry back home, happily chatting until the

elevator door opens to the penthouse, and it's clear by all the yelling coming from Benjamin's room that they're in full terror mode.

The boys don't even notice when Brooke and I move to Benjamin's bedroom doorway, witnessing their fight over controllers.

Caleb and Benjamin are going at it the hardest, doing complicated wrestling moves, but Ethan perks up, no doubt alerted by our weird sixth sense, and shrugs his shoulders helplessly at the brawl before he dives back in.

I clear my throat, and the sound goes unnoticed.

"Benjamin," I say, but he's too preoccupied with the madness.

Caleb, however, drops his hold and smirks when he sees Brooke standing beside me.

"Yes!" Benjamin shouts, holding the controller above his head as a sign of victory.

He turns, and I watch the moment his brain registers who I've brought home with me, then how he nearly falls over at the sight.

"Hi," Brooke says.

Benjamin audibly swallows. "Uh, hi," he returns, waving the hand with the controller in it.

"Brooke and I were just talking about the Christmas gala," I explain before I turn directly to Ethan. "Since Sophia and Caleb are going together, I was wondering if you'd want to go with me, Ethan?"

He looks momentarily stunned, like he can't believe I just outed us like this without talking to him first, but he connects the dots as he catches the staring that's going on between Benjamin and Brooke.

"Sure," he says easily.

"Great," I say, then I give a dramatic sigh. "Oh, but Brooke, I really want you to come, too."

Caleb snickers at my horrific acting skills while Ethan looks slightly amused.

"Benjamin, do you think you could bring Brooke as your date? Then we could all go as a group together?"

Benjamin blinks, like I'm offering him the lottery on a silver platter. "Uh, yeah," he says.

"Great," Brooke says enthusiastically before taking the controller out of his hand and sitting down in one of his gaming chairs. "So what are we playing?"

SEVENTEEN

Given the state of chaos my bedroom is in now, I can't believe I was once embarrassed to have school supplies scattered on the floor.

Considering I arrived here with absolutely no belongings, it's actually kind of impressive how much stuff—although it's mostly beauty products at this point—fills the once-empty space.

Sophia, Heidi, Brooke, and I spend the entire day leading up to the gala preparing.

I thought it would be as simple as swiping on some makeup and curling my hair, but there's much more to it, apparently.

Heidi offered to treat us all to a day at the salon, but I decided I didn't need even more bills racked up on my name—especially when I saw the price tag on the dress Heidi purchased for me—which is why we decided to make a day of it at home.

We do face masks, hair masks, nail painting, eyebrow

tweezing, makeup applications, then finally, we take turns doing one another's hair while they all gossip about celebrity news.

I've never been to a dance before—well, unless the club for Halloween counted—let alone something fancy enough to be called a gala.

When Sophia learns this, she nearly shrieks, demanding details on all my ex-boyfriends—of which there are none—before telling me a few stories from their junior prom last year.

"Are you girls almost ready?" Trey calls through my closed bedroom door. "The car's downstairs."

I finish zipping Brooke into her red strapless gown and step back, admiring how gorgeous she looks. If Benjamin opens his mouth when he sees her, I'm concerned he will drool all over himself.

"Just a minute, love," Heidi returns, sliding into her high heels.

She and Sophia are both in long black dresses, but while Heidi's is sleek and silky, Sophia's is more lace cutouts than actual dress. Heidi's eyes went wide when Sophia pulled it from the garment bag, but now that it's on, it's not as revealing as we all thought it would be.

Frankly, Sophia and her red lipstick could show up wearing a bedsheet and still look glamorous and every bit like she belonged there.

Heidi opens the door, nearly crashing into an impatient Trey hovering in front of it.

"Come on, ladies," he says quickly. "Everyone else is already downstairs."

"I'm going to be fine," Heidi reassures him. "We'll arrive in plenty of time."

He offers her a tight smile and checks his watch every ten seconds as we all pile into the elevator.

On the ground floor, Martha and Rick both compliment us on our appearances, then wish us a good time as we step out into the bitterly cold December wind toward the longest limousine SUV I have ever seen.

"Oh, god," Sophia says, rubbing her hands together for warmth.

Brooke laughs. "That's what you get for wearing that dress."

"Ladies," Caleb says, sticking his hand out to help each of us into the car. "Clean Up Well Five, Avery."

"You don't look so bad yourself," I tell him, hitting his hand lightly before I grasp it to climb in.

He winks. "I know."

My brother, busy sputtering compliments at Brooke, doesn't see the way Ethan's eyes rake over me, but I feel the heat from his gaze.

His slight smile morphs into a full grin when the driver speeds down the street and I barely stop myself from falling onto his lap. I'm already unsteady on my high heels, so I have no chance of maintaining my balance while the car is in motion.

"Hi," I say, trying not to wrinkle the front of my dress—a long gold gown with a deep V neckline—while I sit.

"You look..." He swallows. "'She's beautiful, and therefore to be wooed. She is a woman, therefore to be won.'"

"I don't know if I want to be wooed or won," I say, offering him a small smile.

He reaches up, as if he's going to touch my lips with his fingertips, only to remember that we are very much not alone. "'The lady doth protest too much, methinks.'"

"Methinks you look handsome," I tell him.

His hair is slicked back like he's some sort of nineties heartthrob, and this tuxedo was clearly custom made to make me weak at the knees.

Screw being the next Shakespeare for a living; he should just walk around in formal clothing.

Heidi, Trey, and the Navarro parents each down a glass of champagne on the way to the venue, offering us all sips like it's some sort of adult rite of passage.

Meanwhile, Benjamin and Caleb argued all week about what liquor they were going to siphon from their parents' liquor cabinets to fill the flask I'm sure is in Caleb's coat pocket right now.

The gala isn't too far from the hospital or our building, but it's bustling, like New York always seems to be.

Once we arrive, Heidi is pleased at how everything looks, adorned beautifully with Christmas decorations and lights.

Inside, there's a stage, seating area for dinner, dance floor, and silent auction area, which is a far cry from the way my mom and I spent the holiday season in the past. Usually, we'd pick up as many shifts as possible while trying to snag leftovers and mismade meals from the restaurant kitchen.

Alternatively, on Christmas Day here in New York, we'll start the morning off opening the dozens of presents I've watched collect under the tree, then have a multi-course brunch for the four of us, and eventually, the Navarros will join us for desserts and their annual watching of *It's A Wonderful Life*.

It's tradition for them all to do exactly this, and they all seem enthused that I'm now a part of it.

I can't decide if this is going to be my plan for years to come or if I'll be too busy with school and work in Pennsylvania to make the trip back here.

Plus, there are many things to consider, like how I still need to buy a car, get insurance, and afford gas, let alone make the trek through the wintry mountains that are between here and back home.

Ethan nudges my hand, bringing me back to the present where the adults have been whisked away for introductions, leaving all of us to fend for ourselves at the bar.

Brooke and I outright refuse to allow Caleb to splash liquor in our drinks, but the boys and Sophia have no problem accepting it in theirs.

I'm wildly uncomfortable with the idea of drinking at an event like this, but at least they brought it from home instead of trying to use their fake IDs, which would surely get laughed off in this setting.

Dinner is served after Trey gives opening remarks and thanks everyone for coming and opening their wallets—that line gets everyone laughing—and I hope it will soak up however much alcohol is in their glasses.

After that, it's time for dancing and socializing.

I'm glad it's vastly different from the dancing at the club, and although there are a few people who are doing some sets of complicated steps and turns, most of the attendees are just swaying slightly to the rhythm.

"May I have this dance, Miss Miller?" Caleb asks me, extending a hand.

I blink, surprised by the gesture until I see Sophia is enthralled in conversation with one of the hospital workers, pretending to be fascinated by the structure of the billing department.

Sophia and Caleb have barely looked at each other this evening, and I think he needs a break from their standoff.

"You may, Mr. Navarro," I say, attempting to be equally formal in return.

"Future Dr. Navarro, you mean."

"Who says she won't be Dr. Miller?" Heidi says with an enthusiastic smile.

I don't have time to react to her words as Caleb pulls me to the floor.

He twirls me around with the expertise of a gentleman, which is unexpected considering the last time I saw him dance consisted of him grinding his hips into a girl dressed up as Batgirl.

"Relax, Avery," he says, squeezing the side of my waist.

But I feel plenty of "oohs" directed toward us, and it makes me only that much stiffer.

I don't love the very misplaced attention paid to us, but Caleb Navarro thrives off scrutiny and attention—I guess it's a good thing he wants to be a surgeon.

"You try dancing in five-inch heels and let me know how relaxed you are about it," I bite back.

He slows us down but keeps up the movement. "Should have had alcohol to numb the pain."

I roll my eyes and focus on not tripping over the end of my dress.

"What do you think the worst *Scrubs* quote I could say without context to a group of doctors is?" Caleb asks.

His question is meant to distract me—and it works.

I run through the mental repertoire of lines I have memorized, gliding along easily in his arms as I think on it and biting back a smile when the perfect one surfaces.

"'My god, Barbie, are you a real doctor or a doctor like Dr Pepper is a doctor?'"

He stops the movement between us so abruptly that I slam into him, but he doesn't even notice because he is laughing so hard.

A few people eye us quizzically as Caleb pounds his chest.

"Well done," he says between sputters of waning laughter. "You have earned your break from being my dance partner."

"That easy, huh? Did Batgirl get the same treatment?"

"Batgirl and I did not do much talking," he says smugly.

"Ew," I return as we head back to the table.

"Have fun?" Ethan asks quietly.

"No," I tell him, trying to suppress a smile as I take a sip from Caleb's spiked drink.

"Hey!" Caleb groans, but I'm not sure if it's because of my answer to that question or the fact that I drain his glass.

Aside from their shared looks, Caleb and Ethan couldn't be more different.

Caleb is all clean cut in his appearance, but really, he's the rebel of the two of them, always messing around with Benjamin or plotting some, probably illegal, adventure. Ethan's more calculated and quiet, and although he looks like he'd fit right in at a motorcycle club or on a soccer team, I know he'd rather stay in and read quietly.

But we can all share the trait of laughing at Benjamin's expense, who is doing jolty dance moves around Brooke, who is giggling while trying to maneuver around them.

"Avery, this is Daniel Remy, our Chief of Surgery," Trey says, catching my attention as he approaches with a man I recognize.

I stand as quickly as I can on my heels to shake his hand. "It's so nice to meet you," I tell him.

"Likewise," he says kindly, even though I have the feeling he has no idea who I am.

My enthusiasm spills out of my mouth. "I recently watched a video of one of your more complicated heart transplant surgeries. The one of the seven-year-old boy from Louisiana? Absolutely incredible, Dr. Remy."

"Made possible by nights like these," he says with a laugh. "Are you a new donor?"

Trey laughs at the idea, shaking his head. "My daughter."

Dr. Remy's eyebrows shoot up, but his gaze flicks over the notable resemblance between Trey, Benjamin, and me.

"And, of course, you know the rest of my family, along with the Navarros," Trey says, gesturing around the table.

Ethan actually gets up and offers him a hug, and they chat like they're old friends, talking about Ethan's school plans for next year and what books Dr. Remy is reading right now.

Sensing my stare and silent question, without breaking the flow of conversation, Ethan taps his chest where the line of his scar is.

The realization that it was this man, whose hand I just shook, who performed the life-saving surgery on Ethan makes me want to hug Dr. Remy, too, but I settle for making small talk around the table and indulging in too many desserts.

After I've eaten my second slice of chocolate cake and the raffle winners are announced, the boys circle Sophia, Brooke, and me with devilish looks on their faces.

I'm not sure if I'm eager to find out what's behind it.

"Let's get out of here," Benjamin says coolly.

I shift uneasily, wondering if Heidi and Trey are okay with us ducking out of the event early. "And where exactly are we going?"

"To the after party!" Caleb and Benjamin cheer.

EIGHTEEN

For as much enthusiasm as Caleb and Benjamin had, I expected something more elaborate than all of us crowding into Caleb's room.

Caleb assures Brooke and me that his parents won't be home until at least two in the morning, which seems totally unfeasible to me, but, apparently, it's perfectly normal for them to stay out that late at their favorite cigar and cocktail bar that's a little farther downtown.

Frankly, I'm just happy to be in a place where I can kick off my shoes, but I'm even more grateful when Rick calls to let us know that our pizza has arrived.

Since ordering, the group has split their time explaining to me how New York pizza is the greatest in the world and sharing swigs out of various liquor bottles.

"So, remember, Avery, it's all about the way you fold it to eat it," Benjamin reminds me. "You're still kind of new here, but my sister can't be anything less than a pro at New York pizza."

I follow his instructions, pinching the slice at the crust to form it into a taco shape before I take a bite.

It's definitely thinner yet overall larger than pizza I'm accustomed to, but the only major difference in taste is the red and black pepper Benjamin sprinkled all over the pie when it arrived.

They all watch me chew, eagerly awaiting my review.

"It's good," I say, holding my hand over my mouth as I swallow the first bite.

"Good?" Benjamin scoffs. "The best."

"This one's empty," Brooke says, holding up a pizza box with a confused look on her face.

"They actually did it," Benjamin exclaims to Caleb. "You know what that means?"

Brooke balks at him. "We get a refund?"

"It's Pizza Box time!" Caleb and Benjamin yell while throwing their hands in the air.

"Oh god," Ethan murmurs, shaking his head.

"Do I even want to know what this is?" Sophia asks.

Benjamin pushes the bottles and other boxes out of the way, then drops the empty one in the center of our circle. "Pizza Box is only the greatest game to have been invented in the history of humankind."

"I thought *GoldenEye* was the greatest game to have been invented in the history of humankind?" Ethan clarifies, earning a look of exasperation from Benjamin.

Caleb rifles through his desk drawer, pulling out a few markers and a handful of spare change. "So, anyway, Pizza Box came about when we were visiting my cousin Chris in Toronto last summer. After he got us our fake IDs, he threw us a party in celebration of our very sudden twenty-fifth birthdays. Since we didn't have cards or dice or anything, we got creative."

"And thus Pizza Box was born," Benjamin says, tearing the corners of the box slightly to turn the cardboard into a completely flat surface. "So, essentially, you flip a coin, and if it lands on a blank spot, write in a new rule, but if you land on an existing rule, you have to comply."

"It's like truth or dare," Brooke says. "But it's only just dares?"

Benjamin scoffs. "Don't diminish the game by comparing it to something so common—"

"Pretty much," Ethan interrupts. "But you can write in some truth questions if you want."

"It's actually a good idea," Caleb admits. "I'll go first with the game anyway, since I'm the master of Pizza Box."

He draws a blob in the center of the cardboard and writes TRUTH QUESTION CIRCLE in the center.

"Okay, so if you land in it, ask a question, and everyone has to answer it honestly. I'll start off."

He makes us all go around in a circle and answer his question of "If you could have one superpower, what would it be?"

The game starts off gentle, but I know the more we drink, the worse it is going to get.

At first, the rules are as simple as CHUG FOR TEN SECONDS and ONE MINUTE DANCE BREAK, but Caleb breaks the ice first with more wild rules.

He winks at Sophia before he writes KISS THE PERSON ACROSS FROM YOU, and she retaliates on her next turn by writing KISS THE PERSON TO YOUR LEFT, which in Caleb's case is Benjamin.

I don't miss the gleam in Benjamin's eye at that, not because he's excited to kiss Caleb but because the person on his left is Brooke. She realizes it a few beats after him, and they both blush.

On Ethan's second turn, he lands on BROOKE GIVES YOU A TATTOO, and she makes him stretch his arm across the circle so she can draw a butterfly on the back of his hand.

"Very cute," I tell him, admiring her quick handiwork.

"'So we'll live, and pray, and sing, and tell old tales, and laugh at gilded butterflies.'"

I smile before I flip the coin, then immediately groan.

I've landed on DO A SHOT, one of Benjamin's contributions, for two turns in a row, but I notice that people aren't even waiting for their turn to drink—the bottle is moved as we go, and everyone takes a sip, winces, then passes it.

After me, it's Caleb's turn again, and the coin is equally split between COMPLIMENT SOPHIA and KISS THE PERSON TO YOUR LEFT.

"What happens now?" Brooke asks. "Do you get to pick one?"

Caleb considers it. "Sophia, you are the most beautiful of all my ex-girlfriends," he says.

"I accept this answer," she says. "But I feel I should remind the group that while you have had some sleazy make out tendencies in the past, I am the only girl on earth to actually hold that specific title."

"Cheers to that," Caleb laughs before grabbing onto the front of Benjamin's shirt.

He pulls him into a kiss, and it's not a little peck—it's a full, open mouth affair, and it goes on for at least ten seconds before Caleb breaks it, and the look on his face is incredibly smug.

Benjamin rolls his eyes and wipes his mouth with the back of his hand. "Not bad. Could have done with less tongue, though."

Brooke hands him the bottle of vodka, then leans over to plant a small, somewhat shy kiss on Benjamin's lips. Compared to the one I just witnessed, it's completely G-rated, but I can see it sparks something between them.

I wonder how long they would have tiptoed around each other without Caleb breaking the ice.

"Take One For The Team Five," I whisper to Caleb, who quietly returns it.

Brooke and Sophia are next, giggling hard enough that they can barely pucker for their kiss, then Sophia leans over to Ethan, who turns his head slightly at the last second to earn a smear of lipstick on the side of his mouth.

I wipe it off when he turns to me, and I don't hesitate to give him a soft kiss that I wish could last much longer than it does.

Even in haste—another vocabulary word—the movement of his lips makes me feel warm all over.

When we break, I reluctantly turn to Caleb, unsure if I'm going to get the same treatment as Benjamin, but he thankfully makes a big show of getting on one knee and kissing my hand.

Next, it's Benjamin's turn to flip a coin.

He lands on an empty space and takes a swig from the bottle before writing SMACK CALEB.

"Hey," Caleb says, but even he can't stop from laughing.

Benjamin rolls his eyes. "You could have kissed my

hand, too, you know."

My body still tingles a little from the kiss with Ethan and the liquor that keeps going down my throat.

Everyone around me seems a little relaxed and slightly drunk at this point, but even though I am enjoying the night, I don't want to get out of control.

The rounds continue on with no end to the game in sight.

Brooke makes us all share our most embarrassing moments.

Benjamin has to do push-ups—and it's actually kind of impressive how many he knocks out.

Sophia gets complimented repeatedly.

Almost all of us have to do shots.

Ethan is about to get another tattoo from Brooke, and I'm jealous of the way she can touch him in the group without consequence or raised eyebrows from Caleb.

"Can I do it?" I ask her, holding out my hand for the marker.

She smiles. "Sure."

I don't have a fraction of a percentage of her talent. I can't even draw a good stick figure, but my handwriting is nice enough to stay on his skin for the few days it'll take the ink to fade away.

"Avery was here," I say, turning the period at the end of the sentence into a little heart.

Ethan laughs at the words, then takes the marker from me. "My turn."

While the others are busy arguing over who has to go get another bottle of liquor and snacks from the kitchen, I sigh, relaxing into him more than I should.

He's so warm and inviting, and I'm getting tired.

My eyelids grow heavy as the swipes of the marker tickle my arm.

"Done," Ethan says quietly.

He doesn't announce his presence in my life with words on his skin like I did to him, but there's a small, secretive smile on his face that I know is just for me.

I stop myself from reaching up to trace his lips with my fingertips because, even though the others aren't paying attention to us, that intimate gesture would stand out.

Instead, I force myself to turn away and look at the neat, blocky letters of Ethan's handwriting on my wrist.

"'Your hearts are mighty, your skins are whole,'" I whisper, smearing the letters slightly as I rub my thumb over them.

My eyes drop to the center of his chest, where beneath his scar is his the cavity containing his repaired heart, and his gaze moves from the line on my cheek to my lips.

I swallow, unable to move because the scent of leather and citrus is so comforting and the borrowed Shakespeare words are everything.

"Avery!" Caleb yells.

I sit up immediately, regretting that the moment between Ethan and me got interrupted.

"Focus on the game," Caleb presses. "It's your turn."

I'm having trouble caring about this stupid game now that I'm so emotionally pulled toward Ethan, but I lazily flick the coin just to placate Caleb, landing on CONFESS A SECRET.

I can't even remember who wrote that at this point or

how we ever end this game, but I'm ready for Pizza Box to be over.

"I don't have any secrets," I say, yawning.

The group boos me.

"Not secrets, really, honestly, just stuff you guys don't know about me."

"Like what?" Sophia asks.

I sigh. "I don't know. From my life back home."

Benjamin frowns at my use of "home."

"I know a secret about Avery," Caleb says, slurring his words.

"No, you don't," I scold him, starting to panic slightly at how inebriated he might be.

I glance at Ethan, trying to silently signal him to control his twin.

Caleb laughs hysterically to himself. "Avery eats ketchup on mashed potatoes."

I breathe a sigh of relief, while everyone else seems generally grossed out.

After a beat he casually adds, "And she's dating Ethan."

I don't see how everyone else reacts to this information because all I can see, through my hazy vision, is Benjamin's glare before he storms out.

I get up to try and follow him, but my limbs feel like pudding. I don't think I can get up from the floor, let alone chase him down and try to console him.

Ethan lets out a low string of curse words beside me.

"Well, that backfired," Caleb says with a laugh.

Even though it's not his turn, Ethan moves a coin to the SMACK CALEB space, giving himself permission to reach over and do so.

NINETEEN

Christmas is an awkward affair.

Benjamin hasn't spoken one word to me since Caleb blabbed the truth of what's happening between Ethan and me, but even outside our lack of interactions, my brother is generally quiet.

I feel guilty—and not just for the usual things I feel guilty about—because I've put a damper on the holiday for everyone.

Benjamin's antics are so pivotal to daily life at the Carter apartment that it's kind of dull without him bouncing around and driving the conversation forward.

He doesn't tell Trey and Heidi the reason he's a little withdrawn, and I'm grateful for it. They both try to corner me to figure out what's wrong with him, only to speculate that it must have ended badly with Brooke.

I try to talk to him frequently, but he brushes me off at every attempt, even when I wait for him to come out of the bathroom.

"Avery, just leave me alone, okay?" Benjamin says, not even bothering to look at me as he heads back to the kitchen where Ethan and Caleb are picking at some cookies Heidi and I decorated yesterday.

I officially give up on this holiday and pushing Benjamin into talking to me, calling it an early night before hiding out in my bedroom.

I'm perfectly fine to spend the rest of the evening alone, sorting through the mountain of gifts Heidi and Trey got me, even when the sadness starts to creep in about how the big expectations I had for the day were slightly dampened.

I'm curled up on my bed with one of the many medical bestsellers I unwrapped this morning when Ethan slips into my room, quietly shutting the door behind him.

"Hi," I say, marking the page and setting my book on the nightstand.

As he crosses the room, he pulls a small box wrapped with a red bow from behind his back. "Merry Christmas, Avery."

"I thought we agreed on no gifts," I sputter.

He shrugs and sits beside me. "I couldn't help it."

I pull at the ribbon, then slide open the box, smiling at the delicate necklace inside. It's simple and silver, with a heart at the center. It's blank on one side, and on the other, written in tiny font is—

"'My heart is ever at your service,'" Ethan says. "It's not really that great of a promise, though. Since my heart's been broken and surgically repaired."

"I absolutely love it," I gush. "Will you help me put it on?"

I pull my hair out of the way while he fumbles with the clasp.

"But I really thought we weren't exchanging presents," I whine, turning back to him once it's secured around my neck.

"I don't need anything," Ethan says.

I frown because that's what people should say when a person should have just gotten them a gift.

Ethan's eyes flash. "Actually, there is one thing you can do."

"Yeah?"

"Go out with me New Year's Eve."

"I wouldn't have the first clue of where to take you."

"I'm not asking you to plan it," he says. "I just want you to agree to it."

"This just seems like more of another present for me than for you," I argue. "Unless you agree to let me pay."

"Fine, whatever," he says dismissively. "As long as it means you'll go on a real, formal, official date with me?"

I chew on my bottom lip. "How formal?"

Ethan runs a frustrated hand through his hair. "Are you delaying saying yes on purpose?"

"Who says I'm going to say yes?"

"Avery," he sighs. "Don't delay the inevitable."

I scoot closer so I can wrap my arms around his shoulders. "You've given me your heart, Ethan. The least I can do is take you out to dinner."

"The least?" Ethan says.

Despite the lightness of his tone, there's a darkness in his eyes when he pulls me onto his lap.

At first, I think it's frustration with my teasing him, but

then I realize it's something deeper, more powerful. It's hunger, and it's for me.

His lips crash into mine.

There's no romance, no Shakespeare, no words at all—just him and me, moving together.

Finally.

I cling to his shoulders, desperately clawing at him as I rock my hips forward to increase the friction, kind of like how I did at the club, and the motion causes a low sound in his throat that I definitely want to hear again.

Ethan tangles one hand in my hair while the other slowly moves up my thigh, then hits my waist before slipping underneath my shirt.

I gasp at the feel of his palms on my skin, and he hits a place where no other human being has touched me.

"Avery," Heidi says, knocking as she enters the room. "Oh—"

Ethan and I spring apart instantly.

I jump up off his lap and try to smooth down my shirt while Ethan not-so-slyly moves a pillow onto his lap.

If I wasn't so mortified, I'd laugh at how disheveled he looks, even though I probably look the same way.

I turn slowly to face Heidi, knowing there's absolutely no excuse in the world to justify what she just stumbled upon.

Worse, I don't know what would have happened if she hadn't interrupted.

"Huh," she breathes, gaze flicking between the two of us. "Makes sense."

"I'm so sorry, Heidi," I sputter.

She shrugs her shoulders, dropping the plate of cookies

on the dresser, then turns to leave. "Leave the door open when it's just the two of you in here, okay?"

"Okay," I say, then fall back onto the bed with a groan once she's gone.

Ethan chuckles at my embarrassment. "So, do you want to tell her about our New Year's date, or should I?"

I blindly reach for his hand, and once it's in mine, he lifts it so he can press a kiss on my palm.

It seems like such an innocent gesture considering the position we were just in, but I take it as reassurance that I know I'm going to need to get Benjamin to forgive me, to get Heidi to not tease me too harshly, to get Trey up to speed with this news, if Heidi doesn't fill him in herself.

But somehow, the topic isn't brought up over the next few days.

Benjamin continues to pretend I don't exist, and I don't approach him again at Ethan's advice of letting him cool off.

With Trey and Heidi both home, we spend a lot of time together watching Christmas movies and doing crossword puzzles, but most of all, Ethan and I find a few pockets of time to ourselves to read together.

I think those are my favorite moments, the quiet ones where we sit side by side, lost in our own little worlds but enjoying the ability to share the same blanket or steal a quick kiss when no one is looking.

On New Year's Eve, Heidi, Trey, and Benjamin leave early, off to some party with the Navarros that I am glad to miss.

"You look beautiful," Ethan says as he picks me up.

I laugh because I'm wearing a bulky black winter coat.

There is a lovely red dress beneath it, but I'm not sure when he'll get to see it.

At first, Ethan wanted to surprise me with what he had planned for our date, but I've had enough surprises and unexpected circumstances to last a lifetime. So, instead, we planned out our evening together.

It's not as crowded as I expected it to be in the city, given what I've seen in Times Square every year, but Ethan tells me that's not an accurate representation of the city.

In fact, from my experience, most of what I've seen on television doesn't match up with my expectations of life here.

I know I'm in a privileged bubble, and that's kind of why we planned tonight the way we did. I wanted to spend the evening together, exploring our neighborhood as two normal teenagers out on a date.

First, we go to a tapas place.

I've never had Spanish cuisine before, so Ethan selects a few different dishes—sautéed shrimp drizzled in olive oil, crispy potato slices covered in a garlic aioli, and grilled chicken mixed with eggplant and tomatoes.

Every bite is delicious, and I have one of those experiences where I almost hate to keep eating because it's so good I don't want it to end. But at the very least, I get to savor being with Ethan, alone, for the rest of the night.

After that, we stop in a small tea shop, getting drinks to keep us warm as we walk toward the entrance of the tramway, which runs back and forth between Roosevelt Island and Manhattan.

We swipe our cards and shuffle into the car, and my stomach drops as the cables raise us up into the dark air.

The views are beautiful, and I try to catalog every single building, billboard, and sign I see.

Ethan stands behind me, hands wrapped around my waist, telling me that seeing the city with me gives him a renewed appreciation of how amazing it is to live here.

We disembark to swipe our cards and ride back over to our side of the water, and thankfully, now that I've done it once, I don't have any trepidation about the swaying of the car while we move.

"What's that?" I ask him, pointing to the dock that's just outside the station entrance.

"The ferry."

"There's a ferry here, too? How many modes of transportation can you take in one day?"

"Subway, train, car, taxi, boat, bike…"

"Helicopter," I remind him, thinking of my own entrance, even though I wasn't coherent—another vocabulary word—for it.

"That, too," Ethan says. "In the summer, we'll have to go on a ferry ride all the way to Brooklyn. There are some really cool neighborhoods and parks and stuff that I think you'll love."

"You have until June first," I remind him.

He balks at that. "What do you mean?"

I turn to face him head on. "I've told you before. Once I turn eighteen and I'm no longer—"

"You still really think, after all this time, that Trey and Heidi are going to kick you out or something?"

"I don't think so," I admit. "But…I can't just keep living on their charity."

Ethan shakes his head in disbelief, and I sense underlying hurt in his words. "You have a life here now."

I don't want to argue with him tonight of all nights about all the seriousness that waits for me in six months.

"Can we talk about this later, Ethan?" I ask quietly. "The whole point of our date is just to enjoy each other, and I don't want to think about anything or anyone else right now."

His mouth presses into a hard line, so I stand on my tiptoes, pressing a gentle kiss against his lips.

"Please?" I ask.

"You can't expect me to hold off on this conversation forever, though." He swallows. "I don't even want to think about you leaving here."

I nod, accepting that eventually, we're going to have that talk, and I don't think it's going to end very well.

But for now, I'm happy to hold hands as the snow falls.

We make our way to a French bakery, picking out a mix of macarons and chocolate desserts to share, and then Ethan uses his fake ID to buy a bottle of champagne.

Originally, we planned to head to Central Park to find a tucked away bench to indulge in our purchases, but the snow is coming down steady enough that we decide to retreat home.

"So, this is your room?" I say, shrugging off my jacket.

My imagination wasn't too far off on what I pictured of his space. It's somewhat of a plain room, but there are masculine touches along with the definitive scent of citrus that I associate with him.

There are a few poetry books and a gigantic Shakespeare

anthology on his nightstand, and for some reason, I find that incredibly endearing.

Ethan comes off as this long-haired guy with a rough exterior to most people, but I feel like I get to see the real him, the version that spouts lines written hundreds of years ago, the introvert who doesn't get along with his parents, the one with a dark blue bedspread that keeps him warm at night.

I'm going to spend as much time as possible with him these next six months, worrying a little less and living a little.

"Do you want to go on the terrace?" Ethan asks.

His voice is low and gravelly, and when I turn to meet his eyes, it finally dawns on me that he and I are completely alone in his bedroom—and that he most certainly does *not* want to go out on the terrace or be anywhere but here.

I shake my head and bite back a smile.

Three steps is all it takes for him to get to me.

I don't have time to brace myself as his mouth meets mine. This feeling is unlike any other I've felt in his presence. It's entirely another level of urgent and passionate, and it makes my entire body tremble.

I've known Ethan for such a short time, and there are so many unknowns ahead of us and between us.

But at this moment, right now, I want to be with him, feeling him in every single way possible, baring ourselves to each other, scars and all.

"Ethan," I nervously whisper while he nips my neck. "I want you."

He pulls back, needing to see the certainty in my gaze. "Are you sure?"

I nod, hoping he doesn't notice my shaking fingers that slowly unzip my dress at the side.

"Don't you have a Shakespeare quote for me?" I ask quietly.

I watch the movement in his throat as he swallows, then shakes his head.

And for the rest of the night, there are no words, just actions, feelings, and bliss.

TWENTY

The next morning, I wake up alone, back in my own bed, but my mind is still exactly one floor below.

It would have been nice to spend the night in the comfort of his arms, but even though Heidi and Trey don't have too many ground rules, I know that behavior would have pushed things.

Rightfully so, maybe.

I stayed until after midnight, so we could have one last kiss of the night, the first in the new year, before I snuck back up to my room, smelling of oranges and sugar from the desserts we ate while lounging in his bed.

I stretch upward, and although I'm a little sore, I otherwise feel normal.

Maybe it was a good thing I didn't have any expectations set for what happened between us last night because for the first time I could recall, we simply gave into what felt good and all the new sensations that came along with it.

Being with Ethan, in general, is fairly incredible, but the way we moved together last night...

I can't even find a vocabulary word that comes close to describing it.

After I shower and dress, I head to the dining room to eat breakfast.

Trey and I work through the crossword puzzle together like we always do while Heidi associates the words with various stories and commentary. I don't know if he can sense that there's something different about me, but I catch him and Heidi exchanging a small smile at my good mood.

Ethan and I don't see each other again until we head to school the next day, paired off together behind Benjamin and Caleb, who complain that we're walking too slow.

For the next two weeks, our foursome breaks off into two twosomes more often than not, and time begins to blur together entirely.

Benjamin's still keeping me at arm's length, but he's getting more preoccupied with Brooke and less focused on being mad at me, which I take as an overall win.

In fact, the days are so nice and light that I don't think twice about answering my phone when I see Carol from Social Service's name flash on my screen.

It's the Tuesday-est Tuesday ever, with school, friends, and Ethan—so normal that I don't even consider it should be anything else.

"Hello, Avery, it's Carol from Social Services," she says in her chipper tone.

"Hey," I return. "How are you?"

"Good, good. I was just calling to check in on you and see how things are going with you and the Carters."

I'm surprised that she cuts right to it, instead of indulging in her typical skirting questions, and I wonder, once again, if Heidi said something to her.

"Things are...fine," I say tentatively.

"School? Friends? Homework? Did you end up applying to schools in both Pennsylvania and New York, as we discussed?"

"Yeah," I admit.

I also don't want to seem overeager, like I can't reveal just how good I have it or she's going to make me a case study or put me on a pedestal of some sort.

She starts our normal one-sided conversation, talking about continuing to make forward progress and some resources she has at her disposal to help me.

I doodle in the margins of this morning's paper, where Trey and I got through about half of the crossword before we had to head out, until my eyes land on the date, and then my heart falls into my stomach.

January fifteenth.

My mother's birthday.

Carol, totally unaware of my revelation, still chats away in my ear, and I can't even pretend to be composed when she tries to turn the conversation back around to me.

"I have to go," I tell her, then hang up before I can hear the response.

My mother loved to make a big to-do about birthdays, even though we didn't do much to celebrate them other than light a candle and eat a dessert—that we hopefully snagged for free from the restaurant.

And I'd made it the entire day without knowing it was hers.

I grip the edge of the dining room table, trying to push all the feelings back in, but I'm too far gone for that.

The crack in my armor has been completely obliterated beyond repair.

A mountain of guilt crashes down on my chest, and I can barely stay upright from the weight of it.

I was moving on more with every second, away from the life I had with my mother, the woman who loved me unconditionally, patched up my scraped knees, and raised me on her own.

She sacrificed everything for me, and it took me, what, four months to move on?

I'm completely disgusted with myself, at my ability to be allured by the comforts in this penthouse in the sky, that every single part of me wants to flee.

My chest heaves, and I feel suffocated by the same things that once intrigued me—the closet full of clothes feels like a set of uniforms, the egalitarian design seems like a prison, and the people who have taken me in feel like my captors.

I need to get out of here.

Leaving my mess of homework on the table, I rush down the hall toward the front closet to get my coat. I don't know where I'm going, but I'm desperate to get out.

I push the button on our private elevator repeatedly, willing it to move faster.

When the doors finally part, Trey steps out, and I crash right into him.

"Woah," he says, steadying me on my feet.

I avert my gaze and try to slip past him, but he holds his ground, taking in whatever expression is on my face.

"What's wrong?" Trey asks.

I shake my head and press my lips into a thin, hard line, not wanting to spill anything out.

He sighs and runs a hand through his hair helplessly. "Carol from Social Services called me while I was on the way up. She sounded very concerned."

The elevator doors close behind him, trapping me in this situation.

I take a step back. It's not the way I want to be going, but it's better than standing nearly nose to nose with him.

"Avery, please, you can talk to me," he urges, pleading with me to open up. "Whatever it is, I'm here for you."

Trey is determined to solve my problems, fixing the broken with just one conversation.

But even if that's all it takes, I don't want it. I don't need his or Heidi's help or Benjamin's disappointment with me—I have to get the hell out of here and breathe on my own.

"A car," I choke out.

"What?"

"I need to borrow the car."

He quirks an eyebrow. "Are you in some sort of trouble? Did something happen?"

Finally, I meet his gaze.

I can feel the lifeless expression on my face, like I'm wearing a mask that's slowly draining me of all emotion, and he's the complete opposite. Lines crease his forehead in frustration, or maybe concern, and he's blinking rapidly.

"I need..." I trail off.

My brain is foggy, and I can't figure out how to vocalize exactly what it is I need at this moment other than for him to let me go.

"Is this about school?" Trey guesses. "Carol said that you clammed up when she brought up some details on getting financial help. Heidi and I have already discussed it, and there is absolutely no way we are letting you take this burden alone. Consider it eighteen years of unpaid child support if you need to, but we're covering all the costs and then some."

I close my eyes.

He and Heidi have been too generous already with their time, space, and money. I should be over the moon with this news, but I feel the walls closing in once again.

I don't have the mental capacity to process why I'm reacting this way. "The car," I repeat.

He blinks. "What?"

"I need the car," I say, forcing myself not to cringe at the hollowness in my voice. "I need...to go back."

"Avery, if you want to go visit your hometown, we can go this weekend when you don't have school, and you can get all the closure you need for as many times as we need to go back there."

"Trey, please," I nearly beg.

He sighs. "I don't think you should drive when you're upset."

"Please." My voice breaks. "I have to go today. Now."

He stares me down for a beat, then reaches into his coat pocket, pulling out a set of keys.

"The gold one is a copy of your apartment key. Do you know where our car is in the garage?"

I nod and accept them with shaking hands.

"No matter what happens, Avery, what I said stands," Trey says slowly. "It doesn't matter where you go or what you want to be. You're my daughter. I mourn every single day over the years you weren't in my life, and I hate that the worst had to happen to you for us to find each other, but you're here now. I hope you want to stay here, but it's up to you. We'll support you and love you no matter what."

He turns, letting himself into his bedroom, and closes the door behind him.

The sobs wrack my body, and I sprint to my room, stuffing my phone and a change of clothes into one of the large bags Heidi bought for me.

I pushed back on almost every purchase she made for me, but somehow, I knew it was her way of taking care of me, making sure that although I was in a new space with new people, I at least wasn't wanting for anything.

It's a distinct form of affection that I never experienced with my mother, and it breaks my heart even more.

My determination is renewed, but before I go, I scribble a note to Benjamin, once again telling him how sorry I am and that I'm glad he's my brother, then I slip it under his door before I leave, unsure when I'll come back.

TWENTY-ONE

The drive is tedious.

It's not just because I haven't driven in months or that I'm on the verge of an emotional breakdown, but the winding roads along the Pennsylvania mountains are dark, snow-covered, and a little icy.

For nearly six hours, I grip the steering wheel so hard I think my nails have put permanent marks in the leather.

Most of all, it doesn't give me the reprieve I hoped for to clear my mind.

When I finally show up to the tiny apartment building where my mother and I lived, I'm somewhat surprised to find it's the same as it was, a little rundown yet kind of charming, especially with a dusting of snow everywhere.

The lock on the building door and elevator have been broken since we moved in, so I breeze in and hustle up the stairs to our third-floor apartment.

I rest my head against the front door, giving myself a moment to breathe before I let myself back into my old life.

It's just like how we left it that day before our shift at the restaurant.

My mother's spare shoes sit by the door. Her favorite blanket is folded on one side of the couch. My worn-down backpack sits on the hook. I touch it all, softly, like I'm disturbing a museum of a past life.

I can see the little touches from the cleaning crew Trey hired—my mother would laugh at how spotless the kitchen is and how the bathroom mirror, for once, doesn't have flecks of goopy black mascara on it.

The scent of her cheap floral perfume is strongest in the bedroom, and that's where I end up collapsing, not from emotion but from exhaustion.

I crawl into her twin bed, wrapping myself up in the comforter that still smells like her, and fall asleep.

And when I wake up later, I'm still tired.

I don't think I moved one inch overnight, and although I'm in the comfort of my mother's memory, something doesn't feel right.

It's like I'm hungover from succumbing to my emotions, but I push through the fog while I take a shower and brush my teeth.

I leave my school uniform in a pile and slip on my old clothes, the faded jeans and old long-sleeved shirt that my mom and I bargain shopped for, then decide the best thing I can do for myself is to go see where she's laid to rest.

I need to do this, to get something tangible—or closure, maybe, as Trey suggested—to quell all the thoughts in my mind.

The cemetery is small and attached to a church that she and I had absolutely no connection to, but I see why Trey chose this spot. Her grave marker is beneath a tree, shrouded from the harshest of winter, and set apart from the others.

I should have brought flowers or something to leave here, keeping her company when I'm unable to, but I'm empty-handed.

I dig through my purse, but aside from my wallet, phone, and a pack of gum, I have nothing to offer.

When I see that I have a bunch of missed calls from Ethan, Benjamin, and even Caleb, I take a minute to shoot a text to Trey, letting him know I've arrived okay, then I promise myself I'll respond to the others later.

But first, it's time to focus on my mother.

It's a strange thing to try to connect with a piece of stone on top of cold grass, but I make do.

I open my mouth and let everything spill out—how much I miss her, what my life in New York has been like, how confused I am that she never told me about Trey, the guilt I feel about moving on without her, and all the little things I miss about her most.

And, most importantly, I wish her a happy birthday, even though I'm a day late.

I don't expect to get any kind of response, obviously, since I'm talking to a grave.

But I wouldn't hate it if the wind picked up or some birds flew by, even though it's the dead of winter, just to give me some sort of sign.

The only relief I get is buried deep inside, like the pit of despair that I've been holding onto since the accident isn't actually bottomless.

I allow myself to think of all the good that has come in

these past few months and how proud she would be that I've moved forward with my life—and am now positioned to go anywhere and do anything we could have ever dreamed up.

I don't think there's a better birthday present to give her than that, honestly.

At that realization, I inhale the cold winter air and feel renewed.

It's going to take time to heal completely, and maybe a part of me will always be a little sad for the years ahead that my mother won't be in, but the way to honor her is to adhere to her final words.

"Maybe it's time we both started worrying a little less and living a little more," I say, finally finishing the sentence and making the promise to myself.

I take the long way back to our apartment, driving past the restaurant and my high school, feeling like a tourist in a place I once considered to be home.

I stop by Target, treating myself to a chai tea latte at the Starbucks stand inside, and buy a few plastic bins to help me transport what little belongings I want to take back with me to New York.

After juggling everything back up the apartment stairs, I make quick work of filling them with photos, a few knick-knacks, my mom's blanket, and some clothing.

Every single thing I pack has a memory associated with it—kind of like how Heidi manages to tie most crossword puzzle words to past moments and events—but instead of feeling gutted by the recollections, I enjoy them.

I'm so deep in reflection that I don't hear the knock at the front door until it turns into a banging noise.

I figure it's the landlord, somehow catching on that someone is in the apartment once again and is impatient for an explanation, but when I open the door, I'm stunned.

"Benjamin," I gasp. "What are you doing here?"

"Are you really planning on leaving?" Benjamin asks with a harshness to his tone, pushing his way into the apartment and looking around. "Staying here, I mean?"

I blink. "Oh, uh—"

"Because I'm not letting it happen."

"You're not letting it happen," I repeat.

"We are siblings," he says resolutely, as if we made some sort of unbreakable vow to each other that I'm somehow in violation of at the moment. "We are supposed to fight with each other. And get mad. And protect each other at all costs, and that is happening right now. We are in a fight. I am mad at you. And I'm protecting you from yourself and a horrible mistake."

I've never seen him like this before, so determined and fierce, and even though he's kind of yelling at me, I'm proud of him for doing so.

"Benjamin, I'm so sorry that I didn't tell you about Ethan," I tell him.

"I don't care about Ethan," Benjamin snaps. "I don't care if you date him and break up with him one thousand times or decide to date Caleb or do whatever."

I pause. "Then why are you so mad at me?"

"Because you're supposed to be my sister. We're supposed to have each other's backs and tell each other stuff before we tell other people."

I take a breath, trying to figure out what to tackle first.

"Benjamin. You're my brother, and I love you. But I don't think that's what you actually want."

"What do you mean?"

"Tell me about you and Brooke," I say, crossing my arms on my chest.

He shifts awkwardly.

"Are you two dating?" I press. "Officially?"

"No, we're just kind of...before that I guess," Benjamin admits reluctantly.

"Sharing secret make out sessions and being all shy around each other?" I deadpan.

He squirms at my words, and I laugh.

"Now, do you see why I didn't tell you about Ethan and me?"

"Yeah, I guess so." He rubs the back of his neck. "But I want to protect you, Avery. Just like you stand up for me, Ethan, and Caleb, I want to do that for you."

"You can," I promise. "You can be there for me, just like I'm there for you, but you can't cut me out when you're upset and expect me to be okay with it. I tried so many times to have this exact conversation with you, and you blocked me out."

"Isn't that exactly what you're doing here?" Benjamin counters. "Running away without talking to anyone? Ethan told me you've been planning on moving back here after our birthday."

"For a long time, this was the plan." I stop to gesture around me. "But it isn't my life anymore. My life is with you, Heidi, Trey, and everyone else back in New York."

He nods, and without saying another word, he pulls me into a hug.

We hold each other for a moment until he gets too fidgety from holding still.

"There's one more thing I need to tell you," Benjamin says.

I quirk an eyebrow. "What?"

"Caleb and Ethan are downstairs in the car."

"Did all of you skip school to come rescue me from myself?"

"I mean, it was a tough decision," Benjamin teases. "You know how dedicated Caleb and I are to our studies, but we made a sacrifice."

I roll my eyes. "Wait up here, will you?" I ask him.

He nods, and I bound down the flights of stairs.

Caleb jumps out of the car when he sees me, and I hold up my hand. "Road Trip Five?"

"Road Trip Five," he confirms.

I pull him into a hug, a motion that surprises him, but he returns it enthusiastically.

"Do you mind giving Ethan and me a minute to talk?" I ask him.

"Sure," he says, then leaves me to it.

I slide in the driver's seat, unsurprised that Ethan stares at the dashboard on the passenger's side and not my eyes. The line of his jaw is hard, just like mine would be if he took off without letting me know and didn't return my calls.

"I see you're not a pumpkin," he says evenly, referring to one of our first conversations.

"I think I can survive here for now."

"For now?"

"I turn eighteen in June," I say, the words slipping out of my mouth before I give it a second thought.

"And then what?" he asks curiously. *"You turn into a pumpkin and run back to Pennsylvania?"*

I frown. "Hopefully not the pumpkin part."

"Probably because this isn't permanent," I explain. "I was packing up when Benjamin knocked on the door."

He sighs and leans back into his seat. "If you had answered my calls, I could have been spared from hours in the car with Benjamin and Caleb arguing over music and trip snacks."

"I'm sorry," I tell him.

I try to sound earnest, but the idea of him enduring that is pretty funny, so I allow a few giggles to slip through. The unfamiliar sound of my laugh finally gets him to look at me at least.

I reach for his hand. "I'll try to make it up to you on the drive back."

He threads our fingers together and nods, but I can tell he hasn't completely softened yet.

"And I'm sorry for taking off without telling you," I say. "I was just...really overwhelmed and wanted some space. It was a spur-of-the-moment decision. I should have given you a heads-up, but I had tunnel vision that didn't clear until about an hour ago."

"What happened then?"

"I went to see my mom's grave. Talked at nothing for a little while like a lunatic, but it really helped. I feel okay or at least like I'm going to be okay someday."

"Good." Ethan exhales, like he had a weight on his chest, too, waiting for me to say something along those lines. "But please don't do that ever again. I'm so scared of losing you, Avery. Since the moment you showed up here, I haven't been able to think of anyone else but you."

That terrifies me just as much as it exhilarates me.

"You're like a scar, Avery, that's permanently embedded into my skin," he says slowly. "I feel you everywhere, always."

It's not Shakespeare; it's Ethan Navarro, and in that moment, I realize I'm falling for him.

Or I've already fallen.

It's tough to tell the difference, but it's tangible, like he's already part of me that I can and want to grab onto, so I do.

I lean over and kiss him with everything I have in me until Benjamin and Caleb hit the windshield with a succession of snowballs, and then we have an epic fight in the cold, wet air before we pack up and make the drive back home.

CHAPTER 22

FOUR MONTHS LATER

"This is already going much better than junior prom," Sophia says excitedly.

"And the eighth grade dance," Brooke and Benjamin say at the same time.

Caleb laughs. "Well, the bar is pretty low."

Growing up, prom was merely something I acknowledged as existing—but never had any hopes, dreams, or plans of attending.

I'd overheard gossip about the event by excited upperclassmen and caught plenty of references to it on television, but something about getting all dressed up to spend the night in a crowded, sweaty high school gym didn't appeal to me.

Plus, there wasn't an overwhelming selection of dresses at the secondhand stores my mother and I frequented.

Back then, I could have never pictured this night—or this life.

But here I am.

"'When you do dance, I wish you a wave o' the sea, that you might ever do nothing but that,'" Ethan says, tugging my hand toward the dance floor.

I smile and let him lead me away, then we move together to the beat of the music in sync, an art form we've tried our best to perfect over the past few months.

I've done my best to live up to the promise I made to my mother on that freezing cold January day at her grave, and while there have been moments of guilt and sadness, I've spent as much time living happily as best I can.

This, much to my dismay, included letting Heidi obsess for months over my dress and Ethan's tux, but I knew it was because she wanted me to have a picture-perfect final memory of high school.

Over time, I've grown to love Heidi for how much she cares and wants the best for me, among many other traits.

Ethan spins me in his arms, and I take in the gorgeous setting over his shoulder.

Private school prom, apparently, requires a swanky rooftop venue, and while it's a little ostentatious—one of my recently rediscovered vocabulary words, which was in last weekend's crossword puzzle—I'm not complaining.

We have a full view of the buildings downtown lit up at night, and even though it's not exactly private, a few of our classmates behave like we're in a club.

I see Caleb, Sophia, Brooke, and Benjamin off to the side, laughing together and taking gulps of their punch—which has definitely been spiked—before they join Ethan and me.

The liquid courage seems to be causing everyone to

lower their inhibitions, doing somewhat obscene dance moves in their formalwear.

I spent so much time being reluctant about my life here, and when I finally gave into it and opened up to the people around me, I discovered an entirely new level of love, support, and friendship. It was terrifying but completely worth it.

Thankfully, there weren't really growing pains to work through in these relationships. We just learned how to be together and there for one another over time.

I'm reminded how lucky I am to have Dad and Heidi as my parents every single time Ethan's try to strong-arm him into decisions he doesn't want to make.

Mr. and Mrs. Navarro aren't exactly thrilled that Ethan is planning to attend NYU—and room with Benjamin, to boot—but it's a prestigious enough school that they've chosen to overlook his "unfortunate" decision to major in English.

I ultimately relented on my parents' insistence on paying for school, and although I got a few scholarships to Hunter College to study pre-health, I would save a ton of money by staying with them, at home, while walking to my classes and labs—and occasionally taking the train into New Jersey to visit Brooke at Rutgers.

Caleb is off to Columbia with the intention of actually studying—hopefully with me sometimes—and starting fresh.

He and Sophia are still broken up, even though they're prom dates. They both agree it will be easier to be apart when she's off to California, going straight to work for a major fashion house instead of college.

She flies out next week, which means prom is kind of our last hurrah as a group.

I should be nervous about everything changing just as I'm getting comfortable in my life here, but I'm actually feeling pretty good about what's ahead.

My mother challenged me to stop worrying and start living, and although she's not here to see it, I like to think that each day is in honor of her memory. I just wish she could see me cross the stage in my cap and gown next week.

Which reminds me...

"Hey, Benjamin," I yell over the music and break myself apart from Ethan just enough to face my brother.

"Yeah?" he returns, only slightly dampening his wild dance moves, which makes Brooke roll her eyes.

"You know how Dad and Heidi wanted to give us a graduation present?"

He jerks his arms around like there's an electric current going through his body.

"Benjamin," I say, pulling away from Ethan completely.

I rest my hands on Benjamin's shoulders and gain his entire focus, even though he doesn't stop moving.

"I have a surprise for you."

That, finally, gets his attention.

"Three words," I say clearly. "Joint birthday party."

"Now?" he asks, puzzled.

I shake my head. "At the end of the month. You, me, Heidi, and Dad are going on a trip to Disney."

Normally, this wouldn't elicit any excitement in a teenage boy, but a few months ago while watching television, there was a commercial for some new roller coaster in one of the parks, and it was all he could talk about for a week.

"No way! Are you serious? Are we going to Disney *and* Universal? You know they are two separate places, right? And they're supposed to have that new coaster ready, along with—"

"Uh huh," I interrupt. "All of it. We only turn eighteen once, right?"

He pulls me in for a hug, lifting me slightly off my feet while he crushes me against his chest.

"Put me down," I groan, and he does after he spins us around twice.

"Best sister ever," Benjamin claims, hugging me once more—gentler this time—before he turns back to Brooke to share the news.

"He seems happy," Ethan says.

I grin, then spin around to face him as the music shifts from the techno, hip-hop club beat to a slow song, eliciting a few groans from the people around us.

Ethan's hands hit my waist, and I happily wrap my arms around his neck, tangling my fingers in the ends of his hair.

"Definitely not as happy as I am at this exact moment," I say, pressing a kiss on his jaw.

He pulls me even closer, and we sway slowly together for a few beats.

"Remember the first day we met?" Ethan asks.

"Of course," I say easily. "I don't think I'll ever forget that 'pentathlon' was the first word you ever said to me."

He smiles but moves right past my attempt at humor. "You seemed so broken. And so determined to hold everything in for yourself to deal with, thinking there wasn't anyone willing or worthy of helping you put yourself back together."

Ethan pauses to trace the healed line down my cheek.

"I recognized your scars immediately, not the one on your skin but the ones deep inside you, hiding in a hollowed-out place, because I have them, too. Or had, I guess." He laughs. "Because I think over time, we figured out how to be with each other, to let ourselves heal and open up to all the possibilities for the future. I'm just grateful you let me in, Avery."

If anything, the tear that rolls down my cheek unabashedly is a sign of how much things have changed and how true his words are.

"I love you, you know that?" I tell him.

He shakes his head. "I didn't know, but I sure as hell hoped."

While he kisses me, I put my hand on his chest, feeling his heart pound beneath his own scar.

EPILOGUE

TEN YEARS LATER

The day I met my brother was the best and worst day of my life.

I woke up in the hospital, completely alone and to the physical pain of my injuries as well as the immediate understanding and lucid recollection of my mother's death.

Sometimes, in my saddest moments, I have to push away the last image I have of her, and I always try to replace it with a better one.

The way she smiled at me across the restaurant, even when an angry customer was on an angry rant for something that wasn't her fault. How she insisted on lighting the same candle every year on my birthday—when she got it for my first year, it was panda-shaped, and by my seventeenth birthday, there was barely any wick left. Whenever bills were tight, she tried to convince me that we were simply challenging ourselves to be creative with spicing up leftovers and making meals of whatever was left in the cupboard.

But today of all days, I shouldn't be sad.

I think it's just nostalgia creeping up as Ethan and I enter Carter-Churchill Medical through the front entrance.

We've been away long enough that as the lemon-fresh scent of industrial bleach hits me, all the memories flood back in.

It's not just the accident that I recall, though—I spent four years working in this hospital as an undergrad, putting enough hours in that I could probably still walk through the hallways blindfolded.

"You want to grab something?" Ethan asks, stopping at the entrance to the gift shop.

We hopped on the red-eye from Seattle so quickly I hadn't thought to bring anything to celebrate the occasion. Even though it's not necessary, I don't want to show up empty-handed.

I feel the smile break across my face as I spot one of the large "IT'S A GIRL" balloons, a similar style to the one that Benjamin brought for me the day we met. His gesture set a precedent for his ridiculousness that has transcended the years, and I can't help but purchase it.

It was definitely a strange gesture for him to give it to his seventeen-year-old sister who just endured incredible trauma, but it's perfectly appropriate now, given we got the news about our niece's arrival shortly before we boarded.

As we wait for the elevator, Ethan kisses my hand, lips right over where my wedding band should be.

"I forgot it again," I say with a groan.

"Any other husband would be concerned by this behavior, you know."

He's teasing me because it's almost a normal, everyday occurrence for me.

I can't wear my rings in the OR, so they're usually locked up in my office at the hospital or in my jewelry box at home. But every single day, I still wear the necklace he gave me during our first Christmas together.

I laugh. "'Doubt thou the stars are fire. Doubt that the sun doth move. Doubt truth to be a liar. But never doubt I love.'"

Ethan has been teaching freshman-level literature courses at the University of Washington while working on the first draft of his second novel, which means there are enough books written in Old and Middle English in our house that I've absorbed some of Shakespeare's more famous lines.

And it helps that those particular lines were the ones he said to me on our wedding day.

Ethan kisses my temple as we're lifted to the correct floor, and we walk briskly toward the right room, unable to hide our excitement.

We missed all the drama with childbirth—one of the blessings of needing to account for travel time—so everyone is calm when we enter. It's not quiet, though, because Benjamin is talking excitedly, as usual, and recounting the birth story for what I can imagine is the tenth time.

"Hello, everyone," Ethan calls as we enter.

My parents rush over to us for hugs, and we cling to one another excitedly as I eye the sleeping baby in Brooke's arms while Benjamin beams proudly over the two of them.

"You look great, Brooke," I tell her, rushing to be at her side.

She smiles. "It's the drugs. And that my parents are far away in the cafeteria. Want to hold her?"

"Of course." I tie the balloon to the arm of the chair, pointedly looking at Benjamin. "I figured it was only fair that I repaid the favor."

"Well played," my brother says, pulling out his phone so he can snap pictures of Ethan, the baby, and me.

As I hold her in my arms, my heart soars. She's so perfect, and it's hard to believe that my brother was capable of helping create a child so still and quiet.

Here, in the hospital where my grandparents died, where my father and Benjamin were born, where Ethan's heart was surgically repaired, where a part of me died, my niece lives and breathes.

"Hello, Bailey Collins-Carter," I whisper while holding her in my arms and Ethan holds me in his. "You are so loved already."

We all take turns holding her and making sure that Brooke is comfortable and has what she needs to rest, and once the awe has died down inside me, I notice the two people who are absent.

"Where's Sophia?" I ask.

"In Paris with her latest boyfriend," Brooke explains lightly. "We video chatted about an hour before you got here. She promised she was going to teach the baby to speak French."

I roll my eyes. "And Caleb?"

"Don't you mean, 'Where's the doctor who delivered

this bundle of joy into the world?'" Caleb says, appearing in the doorway.

He pulls me into a hug, then Ethan.

"Doctor Five?" I ask, holding up my hand.

He smacks it hard enough that the sound causes the baby to stir.

"Careful," Ethan warns. "These hands are what keep me clothed, housed, and fed."

He and Caleb start lightly arguing, teasing each other just like old times, and Benjamin jumps in to tell them both to shut up because he doesn't want his baby to pick up any sibling rivalry habits for when baby number two eventually comes along.

I smile at the normalcy of the banter, then at my parents, whose eyes glisten from the emotion of the day. I already know they're going to be wonderful grandparents who spoil the absolute hell out of Bailey.

Sometimes I wonder how life would have turned out if I had been here with them, since the day I was born, but even though we all suffered loss, pain, and hard times, we became a family.

The only permanent reminder of everything I've been through are the memories I have and the fractured line of the scar on my cheek. I still get second glances and questions, but at this point, I don't mind it—it's a part of me, a part of my story, and of Ethan's.

And I'll carry it with me—everywhere, always.

BOOKS BY JENNIFER ANN SHORE

Young Adult Romances

Everywhere, Always

Just Play Pretend

Only You in Everything

Perfect Little Flaws

The Extended Summer of Anna and Jeremy

The Stillness Before the Start

Adult Romances

In the Now

Nothing Personal for Breakfast

This Is Your Life

Young at Midnight

"The Islands of Anarchy" Series

New Wave

Rip Current

"The Royally Human Vampire" Series

Metallic Red

Yes, Your Majesty

FREE GIFT FOR YOU!

Want to make your book an autographed copy? Head over to Jennifer's website and get a free bookplate!

https://www.jenniferannshore.com/bookplate

CONNECT WITH JENNIFER

Hi there,

I cannot thank you enough for reading my work. Truly, it means the world to me!

I'd love to connect with you on social media if you're up for it. I'm on all the major social channels, including TikTok (@jenniferannshore) and Instagram (@shorely).

And don't forget to subscribe to my email newsletter (jenniferannshore.com/newsletter) for bonus scenes, new release announcements, giveaways, and more.

All my love! —Jennifer

ACKNOWLEDGMENTS

This book, dedicated to my mother, has meant so much to me. Not only did I pull in some of our memories and the tone of our conversations, but it was important to me to show the strength of a mother-daughter relationship, not just between Avery and her mom but between Avery and Heidi as well. I've been very fortunate to have a kind, funny, and loving mother and am grateful for her support every single day of my life.

Big hugs to my editing and beta team and everyone who writes reviews for my books. It means the world to me that people not only take the time to read and buy my books but to share and write nice things about them, too.

Specifically, I want to thank the duo over at N. N. Light for their diligence in editing and very generous promotion to help get the word out about my books. Thank you both for your kindness and praises.

Also, special shoutout to Lindsay Hallowell for being such a lovely human and proofreader. I would be lost without your teachings and edits!

I'd be remiss if I didn't give major love to Christopher Meluch, my co-founder of Pizza Box. I'm glad I finally got to work our little (but very damaging and sloppy) drinking game into one of my books.

Finally, I want to thank my friends, family, and husband everything. I love you all very much.

ABOUT THE AUTHOR

Jennifer Ann Shore is an award-winning, bestselling author based in Seattle, Washington.

She writes romance stories that go a little deeper than the standard tropes. Her lineup of more than a dozen books includes standalones, a dystopian series, and a vampire series—with titles such as "Perfect Little Flaws," "Young at Midnight," and "Metallic Red."

Prior to publishing, she led an impressive career in New York, first as a journalist and then as a marketing executive, gaining recognition for her work from companies such as Hearst and SIIA.

Be sure to sign up for her newsletter on her website (https://www.jenniferannshore.com) and follow her on Twitter (@JenniferAShore), Instagram (@shorely), and TikTok (@jenniferannshore).

www.ingramcontent.com/pod-product-compliance
Lightning Source LLC
LaVergne TN
LVHW021659060526
838200LV00050B/2428